SNAKES IN THE PULPIT

FEB 08

CH

SNAKES IN THE PULPIT

Reuben Armstrong

Reuben Armstrong Publishing

Welcome to the
Snakes in the Pulpit Series,
Exposing The Lies And Deception Of Four
Top Mega "Snakes"

Snakes in the Pulpit Series Book 1 of 4
Creflo Dollar is No Stranger to Booty Shaking Women

Coming Soon!

Snakes in the Pulpit:
Bishop T.D. Jakes Denies the Trinity

Snakes in the Pulpit:
Joel Osteen Denies the Lord

Bishop Eddie Long:
Living on the Down Low

For more information log on to
www.snakesinthepulpit.com

Reuben Armstrong Publishing

Dallas, Texas

PRINTED IN THE UNITED STATES OF AMERICA

ISBN-13: 978-0-9798360-0-8

ISBN-10: 0-9798360-0-X

www.snakesinthepulpit.com

10 9 8 7 6 5 4 3 2

"But there were also false prophets among the people, even as there will be false teachers among you, who will <u>secretly bring in destructive heresies</u>, even denying the Lord who bought them, and bring on themselves swift destruction. 2 Pt. 2:1-3:And many will follow their destructive ways, because of whom <u>the way of truth will be blasphemed</u>. By covetousness they will exploit you with deceptive words; for a long time their judgment has not been idle, and their destruction does not slumber."

DEDICATION

This book is dedicated to all whose lives has been jeopardized and hurt from so-called men of God. I also dedicate this book to all false prophets in hopes that by reading this book, it will change your life.

ACKNOWLEDGEMENTS

If you had told me several years ago that I would be a published author, I would have knocked you in the head and said you were crazy. However, when God speaks to you and sends you on a mission, you must act on it. God is the source of everything that I have become.

First, I would like to thank my children and family for their support, and encouragement to follow my dreams to finish writing this book.

Also, I would like to acknowledge the encouragement of everyone who has supported me while writing this book.

ABOUT THE AUTHOR

Taking an unconventional route to gain success in the talk show arena, Reuben Armstrong is a nationally-known television talk show host, and founder and CEO of several successful business ventures. After starting his career as a pizza delivery person, at one of the most recognized pizza establishments in the world, Armstrong realized that he could better serve people by helping people.

Armstrong's true love and affection for the well-being of people led him into the medical field. After years, and countless hours of education and research, Armstrong opened a home health care agency, specializing in helping the sick and the underprivileged. Although Armstrong was helping hundreds of people through his health care agency, he wanted to do more.

Knowing that there was still something missing from his ultimate goal to help people, Armstrong created The Reuben Armstrong Gospel Show, a live radio show. The Reuben Armstrong Gospel Show changed the lives of hundreds of thousands of listeners across the United States.

Due to the overwhelming success of The Reuben Armstrong Gospel Show, Armstrong aspired to take his passion and dedication, of helping people, to a higher level. Armstrong wanted to reach out to the millions of people around the world and show them that he is an ordinary person, with extraordinary dreams of helping millions of people through communication, information, and education.

Armstrong produces shows featuring some of the most influential and well-known entertainers, religious leaders, medical doctors, powerful political leaders, and international dignitaries. He has interviewed respected notables such as Rev. Jesse Jackson, Rev. Al Sharpton, Judge Mathis, Bill Cosby, Lieutenant Governor Mitch Landrieu, and many more.

Through the power of media, Armstrong has created an unparalleled connection with people from around the world. As executive producer and host of The Reuben Armstrong Show, he produces the most anticipated talk show on television. Armstrong entertains, enlightens, and uplifts millions of people from around the world.

"Hi, I am Reuben Armstrong. I would like to thank GOD for all He has done for me. Also, I would like to thank the millions of people who watch The Reuben Armstrong Show. It gives me great pleasure to read your emails and receive your phone calls about the positive impact my show is having on your life. I pray that this book will have an impact on you, as well as change your life."

CONTENTS

What You Do in the Dark Will Come to the Light 21

A Letter From the Author 25

Chapter 1: Bait, Hook and Switch................................33

Chapter 2: Homosexual Pastor 57

Chapter 3: The Booty Shaking Pastor........................71

Chapter 4: "Touch Not Mine Anointed" 85

Chapter 5: The Four Top Mega Pimps 93

Chapter 6: Beware of False Prophets 109

Chapter 7: Jezebel Juanita Bynum 121

Chapter 8: Know Who You Are 131

Chapter 9: Judgment Day Is Coming 137

Chapter 10: Final Words to Bishop Long, Bishop
        Jakes, Pastor Dollar and Pastor Osteen 153

Letters to the Author 157
        The Pimp and the Hustling Spirit..................158
        I Applaud You, Mr. Armstrong.....................172

A Final Word From the Author 179

WHAT YOU DO IN THE DARK
WILL COME TO THE LIGHT

WHAT YOU DO IN THE DARK WILL COME TO THE LIGHT

There is absolutely no one, on God's green earth, who is perfect. Especially the pastors I am warning you about or myself. I am reminded of a passage in the Bible which says, "For all have sinned, and come short of the glory of God," (Roman 3:23). As I read that scripture, I thanked God for letting me know that, I am a sinner and that I can fall short of the glory.

God spoke to me and said, "If you try to hide the mess that was in your life, you will be just like those pastors you are warning people about," so I have to be obedient to God and do what he says, because obedience births Blessings. Amen.

The mess in my life is now a message to others. While growing up in this sinful world, I was charged with a laundry list of charges I am not proud of, but I've repented and so can you.

- Possession with CDS twice (cocaine)
- Bank Fraud (floating checks - charges reduced to theft)
- Issuing worthless checks (writing checks with no money in the account)
- Theft (continued writing bad checks)
- Contempt of court (failure to pay traffic fine)
- Malicious damage to my own property (was dismissed)
- Failure to pay child support (not taking care of my responsibility)
- Forgery (dismissed because the plaintiff was a Christian and dropped the charges).

This is to show you that I am not perfect and we all have skeletons in the closet. No one is perfect except God, and if you trust in Him, He will bring you out of this mess just as He did me. But you have to repent and ask forgiveness just as I did. Just because you have a criminal background, does not mean your life is over and you cannot be successful, as I am now.

As I look back over my life, I ask God why I was so foolish for doing those things and God spoke to me and said "He was molding and shaping me for times like this. You need to now give Me the glory and tell others do not fall for the tricks of the devil." See God will take your mess and make it a message so you can help others. I just want everyone to know how God has brought me from working with the devil to working for the Lord. My past people may hold that against me, but I am not trying to please people, I am trying to please God.

I want to leave this to everyone with a criminal record, or who have even been through similar situations like I have been through, learn from your mistakes, press forward and ask God to guide you. As long as you are obedient and give your life to God, your life will never be the same again. Remember, my brothers and sisters, always be truthful and never lead anyone astray. Tell your story wherever you go. You just might change a life.

A LETTER FROM THE AUTHOR

A LETTER FROM THE AUTHOR

As a television talk show host, I hear some of the strangest things when communicating with people from all different lifestyles. The one thing I have learned is that when I have millions of viewers, and receive thousands of emails from all over the world, there is a huge responsibility that I must embrace and accept.

The media, with its vast reach, bestows a great sense of credibility on celebrities who populate the television airways. I have learned that since I am blessed with an influential voice to those who watch or listen to my show; my voice must be *about* something. When I see something wrong, I must take a stand and be proactive.

If I want to change something that I believe is wrong, I must stand up and make my voice heard. I must attempt to change what is going on. *Snakes in the Pulpit* is a reflection of my life's journey. My words reflect years of personal struggle. Within these pages, I reveal some of the worst—and most painful—struggles of my life. Struggles that went unaided by men of God, men I believed in and trusted with all my heart.

Several years ago, I honestly believed that there was a calling on my life to preach the Word of God. Boy was I wrong! It seemed the more I tried spreading the Word of God, the devil took the form of people— as he often does—who continued to rise up against me. I am now an ex-minister. I resigned from the ministry because I was preaching under false pretenses where the pastor misled me into believing that I was called to preach the Word.

My church home had several thousand parishioners. One Sunday, the pastor and his all-too-conspicuous, four-man entourage invited me to lunch, under the guise of a simple fellowship meeting. However, there was no simple fellowship meal. On the contrary, it was an encounter that changed my life in a profound manner.

The pastor said that he wanted to "break bread and get to know me better." This was a lie that shot straight up from the bowels of hell. The true reason behind the meeting with this *man of God*, and for him I use this term loosely, was that he had decided to call on me to spread the Word of God, stating he saw it in a vision.

Confused and dumbfounded, I asked him to explain exactly what he meant. Without hesitation, he responded that I was "called to preach the Word of God." I grew up in the church, and was very active. My parents were strong and faithful Christians. As fierce as they were in defending their faith, they were equally fierce in supporting me in whatever I pursued in life, as long as it did not contradict the Word of God.

Before departing this life, my parents instilled in me that man could not call you to minister the Lord's Word. God, and only God, has the power and right to make such life-altering decisions. However, the preacher man who sat before me told me the calling was on my life. Even though it did not sit right with me, several days later, when I next spoke to him, I received *the calling* that this man of God said he received in a vision for my life. I knew none of this lined up with the Word of God. Nevertheless, being lost, gullible, and a confused child of God, I fell for his hypocrisy.

I was deceived under his ministry; I could not see the forest for the trees. Because I was faith-filled and badly wanted to expose people to the Word of God, I moved forward with pursuit of my anointing. I acted on the words of man, and not those of the Lord.

After meeting with me and convincing me of his vision for my destiny, what he told me was nothing short of jaw dropping.

"Somehow," he began, "we need to start convincing the people of this church to give more."

Flabbergasted, I asked, "Pastor, what do you mean?" as if he thought there was nothing wrong with what he was trying to do.

The pastor looked me in the eyes and, in a matter-of-fact tone, said, "I am looking to buy this BMW and I need the down payment. In fact, I want to pay cash for it."

I was shocked out of my mind! Naturally, I asked the minister of God what the church has to do with him wanting a BMW.

Nonchalantly, he said, "My brother, I am the pastor. It is the church's job to take care of the pastor. As you continue to grow into this ministry, I will show and teach you how to manipulate these jackasses by using the Word of God." I cannot tell you how astonished I was, and to my amazement, he continued. "Come on, man! We can make some money off these jackasses! We can drive new cars, live in big houses and become rich!" I could not believe what I was hearing from this well-known pastor, a man who had been in the community, and throughout some parts of the United States, with his ministry for more than twenty years.

Several days passed and the pastor had the audacity to ask me why I had not been in church for the past few days. With the same matter-of-factness he had used in dropping that BMW bombshell on me, at our "fellowship meeting," I told him that he might think I am a jackass. I told him that one thing my parents taught me was how to spot a jackass, and he was the jackass that I was warned to avoid.

You see, anyone can be led astray by ill-conceived pastors just as I was. Man can deceive you, if you are not in the Word of God on a daily basis. You must be in tune with God. Many people believe man *is* God. Man is not *my* God. That is a huge part of why I wrote *Snakes in the Pulpit.*

This is from my heart; this is what I feel. Moreover, because one must warn people of things to come, lest one be damned himself, I come to you with this warning: not all is what it appears in this world of swollen, overfed mega-houses of worship.

You can fill a basketball arena with people, but if the Word is not in them, it is not going to do them a bit of good. That is how man, at times, portrays himself as God.

The pastor who convinced me that I was called to minister is now known on a national level. He has thousands upon thousands of members. Sometimes I sit back and wonder how many are being misled under his misbegotten ministry. Consider this a personal message from me to you. Chances are, if you have picked up *Snakes in the Pulpit*, looked past any controversy and have read up to this point, you are also a Christian. You know something is not right in your pulpit.

What you will read in *Snakes in the Pulpit* is very much real. Each chapter is inspired by my personal experiences and the experiences of those I know in the clergy.

So sit back, relax, and enjoy reading what God has laid on my heart.

Thank you…and God bless you.

"Then the LORD said unto me, The prophets prophesy lies in my name: I sent them not, neither have I commanded them, neither spake unto them: they prophesy unto you a false vision and divination, and a thing of nought, and the deceit of their heart"

—Jeremiah 14:14

BAIT, HOOK AND SWITCH

CHAPTER 1
BAIT, HOOK AND SWITCH

Many people attend church or join ministries for different reasons: to get answers, change their lives, or seek counseling. Unfortunately, for the past several decades, the evangelical movement has been more heavily supported by marketing than anything else. As a result, many churches will broadcast programs or commercials as bait to lure the most vulnerable people through their doors.

Pastors know that once these unsuspecting lost souls come to visit, they will probably join their churches or get involved in their ministries which translate into more money in the pastors' pockets for fancy cars, expensive homes, and designer suits. It's really a shame pastors spend countless hours researching and studying how and what to promote to build wealth, fame, and fortune for themselves.

They may advertise how they can help you save your lost soul, mend your marriage, and even show you how to live a prosperous life just to lure you into their royal palace they call "church." The truth is some of these ministries have no intention at all of doing anything they promise.

Unfortunately, believers not only fall for this act, but are also unknowing and unwilling participants because they don't see how these pastors and church leaders are deceiving their members. The believers' faith is so strong and they want to believe so badly, that they merely become part of the deception machinery.

Ministries no longer use traditional methods such as personal invitations by church members or a simple signs on the front lawn displaying the service times and the subject of the sermon to get people into church. Now, they're using giant electronic billboards which pop up not so coincidentally in well-to-do neighborhoods. Obviously, this is no coincidence. These signs can be seen down the block as a sign of a wealthy, 'happier' lifestyle.

Many churches are now building gymnasiums, schools, and even supermarkets and restaurants in what is looking less and less like the House of the Lord. To be sure, many ministries don't care to spell out every single detail of what they are all about and their motives in their advertising.

Most promotions don't contain much detail, which is a tactic designed to mislead potential tithe payers by promoting one thing (baiting) and presenting something entirely different when someone answers their ad (switching).

Once these houses of 'worship' get people within their hallowed halls, the much-wanted worshipper is besieged by a mangled mess of scriptures twisted in such a way that they mean exactly what pastors want them to mean. Sad to say, most people in the body of Christ don't have the spiritual discernment to know that they're being deceived because they don't have the biblical background to know how to properly interpret the scriptures that the pastors are presenting to them.

Believe it or not, pastors are manipulating true evangelism to hook members into their churches. The most ridiculous example of this I have ever seen takes place in Europe. A group of "missionaries" who didn't speak the local language were squatting down, waddling, and quacking like ducks in the city square while handing out slips of paper. People who took the flyers discovered they had just received a tract about Hell. I wanted to call them quacks before they waddled off, but I couldn't get a word in edgewise! Well, I guess here in these pages lies my second chance: You people were quacks! There, I've said my piece.

The upshot is that while many of these deceptive pastors and church leaders drive Phantom's and Mercedes and live in towering mansions, they're teaching the body of Christ that God wants to bless them, but with conditions; such as they have to give "seed" money to the church and God will shed blessing according to what they have given. According to the Bible, God does want to bless His followers But, in reality, the pastors are the ones being "blessed" so to speak, because church members are being asked and chastised to give more and more beyond their tithes. All the while, these 'men of God' are using the Holy Scriptures to justify the masks they wear in order to portray a credible, vibrant church body. Often it is the pastor being worshipped instead of God.

The bottom line, however, is that it's all about money. Not revival. Not worship. Not the Word, but Money. To accomplish their ruse, some of the ministry team is dispatched to homes and use special bait to make it seem like they care about you.

There are websites that show pastors how to target a church audience. Many ministers will even go online to purchase a packet to teach themselves how to start a church and target potential members when God has never called them to spread the Word. It is truly reminiscent of any pyramid scandal or mass-scam accessible by any two-bit web crook looking for the blueprint on how to make a quick buck. How is this any different than your average $19.99 ad? It is truly representative of a processed, fast-food mentality when it comes to religion.

Make no mistake: These self-appointed pastors will be sent to Hell. If you're a Christian, and you believe the basic tenets of the Bible, if you believe the Lord despises deceit, blasphemy and misrepresentation of His word, there is no other logical conclusion to which one could come. Such sites as the aforementioned explain that pastors need to target potential members' needs, hopes, joys, and struggles; in other words, focus on what's important to them in their own lives, and learn how to speak their language so that they can connect to potential parishioners both personally and spiritually. In reality, however, they only want to connect with the pocket books of the parishioners.

While on vacation in Georgia, I got lost and couldn't find a place to go for help. Every time I turned my head I saw a church, but no one was there to help me or answer questions. When I needed help, no one wanted to connect with me. Why? Because they knew I wasn't going to become a member any time soon of THEIR church. I was just passing through. "What would Jesus do?" It's become as popular a catchphrase as "where's the beef?" Well, in this case, I'm pretty sure Jesus wouldn't leave a stranger hanging when he was in need of help right outside the house of God.

So, then, why are the churches doing this if they don't want to meet people's needs? Because they're focused on getting large numbers of intelligent, moderate- or high-income people through their doors so they can contribute to the royal families ('pastors') wealth. It's all a vicious cycle of recruit, retain and re-up, really. Recruit the "jackasses," retain their membership through false promises and have them re-up the ante each month. It's the worst form of fleecing. In reality, these pastors don't care much about meeting people's needs, other than their own. These pastors are so low that they stoop to use the Word of God for fame and fortune.

These 'people' pull and maintain crowds with spectacular displays and then hit them with an insensitive, pushy presentation. Believe me, these snakes know how to entertain the masses in their royal palace arenas. Some pastors invite members to their home for Sunday dinner to supposedly get to know their families. I've seen these "invite" many times myself. Trust me, it happens. Many times, what they really want to know is how much money you're making and what kind of cars you drive.

There are certain questions they'll ask during these

sit-downs, questions they know they can slide past a person when they're feeling relaxed in these huge, palatial estates. If a parishioner is making "good" money, they would automatically "move up the ladder" in the church. Connections and politics play a huge role in the outside world. Don't think for a second this mentality doesn't penetrate the palace walls. A person may even become a minister, even though God has never called them to that position.

But, God forbid anything should ever happen to your income. Some of these fires filled, holy ghost churches will drop you like a rock and pray you get up from the hard fall if you're in need because the mega snakes (pastors) aren't nearly as interested in people without money. Yet, some people are so deceived that they continue to pour out their hard-earned money to the point of falling on financial hardship, all so that these snakes will pay attention to them and acknowledge them as "givers."

The truth is, the pastor may give you numerous reasons why you need to "sow your seed to the Lord" in tithes and offerings over and above what your financial position will support, but many believers and unbelievers alike have been led astray and lost everything they owned. Entire segments of church are earmarked particularly for laying guilt trips on members. 'Don't give me the money,' they say. 'Don't think this is about me,' and 'It's your soul we're trying to save.'

The bottom line is this: We need to ask the question, "Do these pastors really care about people getting saved, or are they running money-making schemes to fatten their wallets?"

According to Forbes.com, four top mega pastors can answer that question if they are not sitting in their easy chairs in their several-million-dollar mansions, or flying the friendly skies in their million dollar private jets. Get a load of the worldly possessions of some of these men of God: One pastor operates a music studio, publishing house, computer graphics design suite, and owns a record label. Another money-making pastor has a record label, a daily talk show, a prison satellite network that broadcasts in 260 prisons, and a twice a week web cast.

A third pastor drives a $350,000 luxury car, lives in a $1.4-million, six-bedroom, nine-bath mansion on 20 acres, and has a chief operating officer and a special effects 3-D website that offers videos on demand. Lastly, a fourth pastor who quit college because he saw the church as a money-making opportunity, to help his father continue to mega his pocketbook, has a four-record deal and spends $12 million on annual television airtime. But at what point do blessings from our Lord become symbols of personal greed and excess. Oh, I'd say sometime around the first payment being made on pastor's new Lamborghini.

By the way, have you ever noticed that once pastors make it to the top and can afford all the fine luxuries of life, they forget about the laypeople that supported the ministry from the ground up? Some pastors are even surrounded by security, and no one can get to the "royal family."

They come to their church with their entourage, and the only ones who can get close to them are those who are willing to "serve" them, or those who come with money or connections to wealthy and famous people. Does this not remind you of your typical rapper or professional athlete? At least those people let you know where they stand, and don't solicit money from you to afford their entourage. Magically, when visitors of note in the community, such as a mayor, councilman or state representative show up, the entourage parts and these people have a clear, unfettered path to the high and mighty man of God!

Are these preachers of faith practicing what they preach to you, or do they stand at the lectern and think they are gods? If you want that question answer I am sure Pastor Dollar will address that as he preaches "we are Gods." The first commandment in Exodus 20:3 is, "Thou shall have no other gods before me." 1 Timothy

6:10 clearly states that "the love of money is the root of all evil." If you look at the countenance and attitude of some of these frauds, sometimes the word 'humble' doesn't come to mind.

An article on MSNBC.com features a pastor who was charged with defrauding his own church out of $1.2 million in insurance settlements, to say nothing of the fact that he bought a $300,000 airplane out of the church's account. In relative terms, this is a drop in the bucket compared to other, more nationally and world recognized mega snakes. That $1.2 million seems like a welfare case compared to the hundreds of millions being bilked from congregants of mega churches.

Welcome to the church business, where mega snakes often act as chief executives and use business tactics to grow their congregations. Do not fall for these snakes. They will deceive you right in your face. And there are so many of them in today's churches, it's become an epidemic! Remember, Satan was pretty tempting to Eve with that apple in her face. The pastor may look sharp, exhibit a fiery preaching style and even speak in tongues with the best of them. He might even preach really well, he may come to your house, call you every week, but all is not as it seems. Let's not forget the praise and worship leader. You love to hear him or her sing special music every Sunday morning. But guess what? Yep, he or she is a snake! The same breath that person uses to glorify the Lord in song is the same one he or she uses to backbite every member in the church by gossiping about who's sleeping with whom and which woman is screwing the pastor.

Again, I've seen it. And I've spoken to others within these congregations and choirs who have seen and lived through it. But don't take my word for it. Ask people in similar situations and positions in your church what they think of this. Those who are honest will tell you no different than I. That is, if you can find honest people in the church.

Ready for yet another shocker? Have you ever gone through a financial hardship to the point of meeting with the pastor and the finance committee? They tell you that they can only give you a certain percentage of money, right? That's because they're taking the rest of it for themselves. While they are counting the money that was given to the Lord, please do not take this personally. This is how snakes strike! They bite you and squirm away. And these snakes really prey on people with financial struggles. Again, snakes have no conscience. Why should they care?

Snakes really prey on people with marriage struggles, as well. Here's a true story about a married couple who wanted a divorce because they were struggling over a financial problem. Hopefully, none of you reading this book can relate to the following scenario. If you can, I'm genuinely sorry. Jane and Paul had been married for seven years, and had not been in a church for more than three.

While sitting at home one evening discussing which property each person wanted to take after their marriage had been dissolved, they saw a church commercial on television (which was turned on as "background noise") that advertised, "If you're broke, I have what you need. If you need healing, I have what you need. If you want to put your marriage back together, I can help you mend it."

The underlying message was that the church had what these people needed, and all they had to do was to come to the church and receive what the pastor had to offer. Remember, Jane and Paul knew that their marriage was about to come to an end unless they sought help. Desperation leads to unhealthy, non-thought out actions at times. But when you've reached that last level of desperation, the irrational becomes rational.

What was once unthinkable becomes thinkable. Funny, how so many come to the church once they've reached the point there's no where else to go. In this couple's desperation, the commercial caught their attention. Jane and Paul began talking about possibly seeking marriage counseling at the church. But several Sundays passed, and the couple didn't seek help.

There was one Friday afternoon when Jane was working in her flowerbed when she heard a voice say, "Hello, my sister." "Good evening, Pastor;" she responded, as she looked up and saw Pastor John and some of the church members standing there as walking witnesses to the community. "Pastor, I've been watching your church broadcasts on television. Your church really knows how to praise the Lord," she said. And so the false idol worship begins. Fully and emotionally invested in what this snake represents and what his very presence before her means, Jane is now dancing and shouting all over the neighborhood as if God, Himself, had just made Himself visible to her.

She is elated because she's happily talking to the man on television who can fix all of her problems, right there in her front yard! What an enticing opportunity for a snake bite. "So, what brings you out this evening?" Jane asked Pastor John. "Oh, just out blessing the community," the pastor responded. "Are you a member of a church?" "No," Jane said, "But I've seen your commercials saying that you can solve my marriage problems."

It is a proven fact that these snakes target women more than men because they believe women are more vulnerable. They know that men can usually see through another man's lies. Unfortunately, this also explains why on any given Sunday, you'll see many more women than men in a given church. Pay attention; look around any church you visit from this day forward. Who's doing the hooting and hollering and foaming at the mouth in the first three rows? Do you see more ties or purses in the pews?

A real man knows whether another man is someone of good character or whether he is just after his wife. At any rate, Jane was so impressed, and just as importantly, so comfortable with this serpent that she began telling him all about her marriage and financial problems and that she would like his counsel. So, Pastor John invited Jane to come to church on Sunday. She agreed.

Later that evening, Paul came home and she told him the good news that Pastor John had dropped by and invited them to church on Sunday. Remember though, Pastor John only invited Jane to church. Paul was nowhere in sight, and the pastor never even mentioned him. Is this a simple case of out of sight and out of mind? I think not!

Sunday morning came, and they went to Pastor John's church. When they arrived, the church was packed with cars all over the spacious parking lot. When this young, faith-driven couple walked through the church door, they were welcomed with arms opened wide. The greeters were very polite and smiling. One of the greeters asked, "Are you a first-time visitor?" "Yes," replied Jane.

The greeters, or "greeders" as they could really be called, grabbed Jane and her husband by their hands, and asked them to fill out a visitor's package for the church record. Included in the package was an envelope for tithes and offerings. One of the questions on the visitor's card was, "Is this your first time visiting the church?" When Jane and her husband gave the card back to the greeter, she immediately noticed that Pastor John had invited them. So, she alerted the pastor's security team, or body guards, that Jane and Paul were in the congregation. Now, the snake is preparing to bite.

Since the pastor knew that others like Jane would be coming that Sunday because he had just been out "witnessing" in her neighborhood, he preached about how to develop a good and prosperous marriage. See how the snake is using the Word of God to bait you in, to manipulate and deceive you like he has the answer? Remember those Internet sites that serve as a 101 course on discerning what people are concerned about and focusing on those concerns and harping on them for profit?

Well, it was obvious this pastor had either read or written them because here they were being acted out right there in church. The fact is millions upon millions of people worldwide are listening to these preachers and believing everything they say. And people are spending millions upon millions of dollars they can't afford to spend, all because they're being hoodwinked, bamboozled, led astray by mysterious spirits. Satan is the ultimate master of deception. He will lie and find a way to make you believe it, IF you are not grounded in the Holy Word of God.

People, please, I beseech you; please be aware of false teachings. Test what you hear against the Word of God. Do not just take the preacher's word. Read the Bible for yourself, and pray for God, Jesus, and the Holy Spirit to enlighten you to the truth, as He would want you to be.

The problem is that some preachers such as Bishop Long, Pastor Dollar, Pastor Osteen and Bishop Jakes are so convinced today that they have power and assurance of a happy, prosperous, healthy, problem-free life that they have fallen into Satan's traps. Of course, these same snakes will tell you until their blue in the face that it's not about them. They are far from cocky or self-righteous. They are too God-fearing to put themselves on the same level as their God. God made it clear that Satan would search us out, look for our weaknesses, and use them to lead us into a false sense of security in order to make us even more susceptible to his leading us when we don't even realize it.

Satan used Moses' temper against him so that he would get angry and strike the rock instead of speaking to it as God directed. Satan also used the beauty of a woman to entice King David into murdering her husband and taking her for his own wife in 2 Samuel 11. And Satan even identified the mighty Jacob's weak spot, which was money and riches. Satan has deceived people, kings, and even entire countries. Why? Because he has come to steal, kill, and destroy according to John 10:10.

According to the Scripture, Ephesians 6:10-12 "Finally, be strong in the Lord and in His mighty power. Put on the full armor of God so that you can take your stand against the devil's Schemes. For our struggle is not against flesh and blood, but against the ruler, against the authorities, against the powers of this dark world and against the spiritual forces of evils in the heavenly." I guarantee you that if you don't put on the full armor of God, as it is stated in Ephesians 6:10-12, Satan will buffet you with temptations based on your weaknesses and lead you down a broad, easy path of destruction which is far removed from the narrow path of Christ. Even if you do develop yourself in the Holy Word, you can still be caught up in these snares that the Devil throws at you. So how much more will he do so if you are not protected by the Word? Satan has a gift of making the narrow path that leads to life look amazingly much more difficult than it is. Christians are even more susceptible to Satan's attacks than nonbelievers.

After all, why would Satan tempt people he already has? But for those who are washed in the blood of the Lamb, Satan tries even harder to wretch them. He must employ his full battery of lies, fleshy temptations and demons to win over these innocents away from the Lord's Kingdom. Even Paul, oftentimes called the greatest of the Apostles, was tempted by Satan. Second Corinthians 12:7 says: "And lest I should be exalted above measure through the abundance of the revelations, there was given to me a thorn in the flesh, the messenger of Satan to buffet me, lest I should be exalted above measure."

We need to WAKE UP and live by the examples and directions the Bible gives us. And the fact is; many churches and pastors such as Bishop Jakes, Bishop Long, Pastor Osteen and Pastor Dollar preach the virtues of money and prosperity, which contradict the teachings of scripture. Didn't Jesus walk the earth almost in rags? You don't think Jesus could have at any moment gone out and draped Himself in the finest of apparel of the times? So, what makes these modern-day preachers and bishops any better than the Christ, the Son of the Most High God? I'm not saying they should be poor, or live from hand to mouth.

Many reading this book will no doubt counter its message by saying pastors preach prosperity, and having prosperity isn't against the teachings of God. The Lord blesses those who keep and preach His word. But to flaunt their wealth and riches (their bling bling) in the faces of some of the members of their congregations who live on welfare, blatantly contradicts the Word of our God. There's a place for everyone and everything in the world and a place for mega churches and mega pastors, as well; but churches that promote this modern health, wealth, and prosperity gospel agenda may already be doomed.

How do I know all this, you may ask? What in the world gives me the guile, the audacity to make these claims? Good old personal experience. I was that member who got promoted to minister when God never called me to the position. The story of Jane and Paul is based on a true story about how my best friend marriage was torn apart by a snake pastor.

As I look back on all of it now, I knew there were so many things going on in my church that were wrong, but I was too afraid to acknowledge them. I knew of pastors having sex with the deacons, and members of the finance committee stealing the church offering. Nevertheless, I kept showing up Sunday after Sunday anyway. I guess a few others have seen the light since then, as well. I still believe there are good men of God out there. Believing otherwise would be a clear sign of lack of faith in my God, Who can change all things for the good.

My Lord is good. He's looked past my transgressions, including those I've committed unknowingly while under the spell of the snakes. I'm now under excellent leadership at the local church where I am currently a member. Unfortunately, the more we continue to feed some of these money-making hogs (or snakes), the more they want. It's a kin to pouring more than a little kerosene on an already blazing inferno. When we, "give, give, give," the question then becomes, "What do we get back?"

Some preachers make it seem like God is blessing them with all of their money; but in truth, it is not God, but the people in the pews who are filling their pockets. The ironic thing is the pastors' wealth is then used to illustrate to the congregation that they themselves can be prosperous. Then we give even more and the vicious cycle continues. Pastors will never tell you that, however, because they want to create a sort of mystery about where the money comes from.

It's all a game preachers play, and these days, you have to have a personal relationship with God, or you will never have the discernment to recognize the game!

The fact is, the only reason a prosperity message works is because we live in a materialistic society where the average church member is more focused on making money and earning great wealth than he or she is with the Lord.

That's why the pastor can preach messages like, "If you give to the church, God will richly bless you," and you'll keep giving to get the material blessings you think are on the way. But nowhere in Scripture does Jesus promise material blessings. Ephesians 1:3-4 says "Blessed be the God and Father of our Lord Jesus Christ, who hath blessed us with all spiritual blessings in heavenly places in Christ. According as he hath chosen us in Him before the foundation of the world, that we should be holy and without blame before Him in love." Jesus promised us "every spiritual blessing in Christ." Now, if He gives you more money, great! If He blesses you with a big house, great! More power to you! But my point is, nowhere in scripture does Jesus promise that everyone who gives to the church will drive a BMW and live in a mansion.

Notice also that the Ephesians passage says that we are to be holy and blameless before Him in love. These days, brothers and sisters, we cannot make the mistake of simply allowing SNAKES (pastor) to teach us how to get to that point of holiness and swallow everything he says. He may, in fact, be leading you astray. He's only a man. Do not Worship the man!

That's why we all need to have our own walks with God. These walks should be intensely personal ones. God is the only One who can get us to the point of being holy and blameless before Him in love. We need to be that way, even if our leadership isn't.

"For the time is coming when [people] will not tolerate (endure) sound and wholesome instruction, but, having ears itching [for something pleasing and gratifying], they will gather to themselves one teacher after another to a considerable number, chosen to satisfy their own liking and to foster the errors they hold,"

—2 Timothy 4:3

HOMOSEXUAL PASTOR

CHAPTER 2
HOMOSEXUAL PASTOR

This is not breaking news. Sad to say, some Pastors such as Bishop Eddie Long do sleep with members of their own sex; some even believe in same-sex marriages. They certainly won't mention this in public and most won't even bring up the subject unless the content of that day's sermon means there's no getting around doing so.

I was talking to one snake that identified himself as "living in the closet," or "living on the down low." This self-professed "man of God" told me that when he wants a man, the first place he looks is in his church. Among the places that are most fruitful in producing gay brothers, he said, were the deacon's board and music department. I'm sure some of you reading this book will keep a closer eye on the members of those church groups from now on. Or have you noticed this trend already? Come on, now! You *know* Brother Jerry dresses just a little *too* nicely!

This gay "man of God" went on to tell me that the music department in particular was fertile ground for homosexual activity. Music is commonly known as an outlet where brothers can express themselves in...let's say "a spirited and flamboyant manner."

These African brothers are attractive and muscularly built; many have exotic tribal voices that get the sisters excited. Of course, the silent down-low brothers in the congregation love these African visitors for the same reasons. Both fall for these brothers because of their physical attributes; they really do not look further or consider whether these brothers are of marriageable quality. This shouldn't surprise you. With the almighty dollar seemingly ruling our every decision and reaction these days, and with a scarcity of eligible brothers out there, some sisters believe if a man isn't in jail or on the pipe, he's "...the one." As I like to say on my talk show, "...this is real talk."

There have always been men on the "down low." If you want proof, ask Bishop Eddie Long. I'm sure he can answer that question in a hurry. The problem is this, the HIV threat makes the deception of these brothers disturbing, deadly, and just low down. I can't help believing that most men who have sex with men on the down low are simply too ashamed or too afraid to admit they're actually homosexual. Regardless of how far we have come as a people, the stigma associated with homosexuality is still too much for some men.

Remember years ago, when the gay lifestyle was openly condemned and some even made fun of boys who appeared to be feminine? Today's political correctness machine has extended its far-reaching influence into this area of our lives, as well. Today it's frowned on to make a public statement that is in disagreement with the homosexual lifestyle; it's just not "right" to do so.

As Christians, we're also afraid it will look as though we're hate mongers if we tell our children this practice is just plain wrong. Forget about the fact that the Good Book disowns homosexuality and denounces the lifestyle choice as unholy and an abomination. Just ask Trent Lot's wife. She'd agree. There are many reasons people may come to lead a homosexual lifestyle, but I believe it is a conscious choice.

Children these days are raised in single parent homes without the on-going presence of a confident heterosexual male; many have pastors and friends who introduce them to the gay lifestyle. There are homosexual youth pastors who claim they are taking youngsters on a trip to sing or to perform…but when they return, some child has been sexually abused.

We parents are not taking the time to *listen* to our children. Sure, our lives are busy; we work hard to make ends meet and take care of our families. So yes, it's hard to spend quality time with our children. But you might be shocked to find out what really goes on between a youth pastor and your child. Don't get this twisted; just because he's supposed to be a man of God and a respected person, doesn't mean that he won't succumb…and it could be your son or daughter he's fondling. I have witnessed youth pastors telling parents that they were taking the young boys and girls for pizza, only to find out they were in a motel having sex. Beware, beware! Just because he's the youth pastor, *do not assume your child is safe.* Parents today don't seem to have much concern where their children go or what they are doing. But I say parents should *always* be concerned and *involved* in their children's lives.

There appear to be a great many hypocrites in black churches. I'm sure this extends to churches of other races, such as the one headed by Joel Osteen. But I'll speak only of the churches with which I've had experience. No one — I mean *no one* — hoots and hollers, foams at the mouth and kicks their skirts up in the air and says he or she loves Jesus as much as the black church. And it is this which makes our churches the biggest practitioners of hypocrisy! Who else has such a knack for having little old women catch the Holy Ghost in the front row, while at the same time the deacons in the back are skimming from the building fund and the usher in the restroom playing with little girls during services? The same shady liars who preach against and condemn homosexuality are the same liars who are likely to be sleeping with the deacon or usher. I will go so far as to say the associated pastors and even the praise and worship leaders may be involved!

Since this down-low phenomenon has been in the media lately, women have begun to play detective, checking up on their men; straight brothers are walking a little straighter. Meanwhile, the down-low brothers are spreading AIDS as freely as if it were Halloween candy. This is not a plot against Bishop Eddie Long or the down low brothers, people; homosexuality is a sin! And if you're not against it, then you are an *enabler*; by turning your head and refusing to face facts, you enable it – you allow it to continue. It's exactly the same as buying a drink for a known alcoholic. You're an enabler. You're enabling the problem to continue. Get a clue, Body of Christ!

A study shows the large rate of HIV and AIDS in the homosexual community is being mirrored in the black community. (Watch out Pastor Dollar and your floozies.) This may not seem dramatic, but if we continue to advocate same sex marriages, eventually our population will decrease until there is no one left on earth! What kind of gift would that be to leave to our great, great, great grandchildren? A world where the few people left on the planet are those who simply have yet to die from a still-incurable plague? Do you think HIV and AIDS will be cured any time soon by a medical community which has yet to find a cure for the common cold?

The last time I checked, two people of the same sex could not conceive a child. We are headed for destruction, and we're so caught up in the "here and now" of political correctness and oversensitivity to peoples' feelings that we're overlooking this simple reality.

Ted Haggard a nationally-known pastor wrote a letter to his mega-church admitting that he was "a deceiver and liar" who had given in to his dark side, confessing to sexual immorality. The snake apologized, saying "Because of pride, I began deceiving those I love the most because I didn't want to hurt or disappoint them." What he really meant was he didn't want to hurt or disappoint the *thirty million* true believers he had *brainwashed.*

The bottom line: he preferred the feel of a penis inside his rectum and his wife didn't have the right equipment to please him. Of course, saying that would not have been appropriate in his very public apology…an apology designed to foster public sympathy and support. The snake then said, "The fact is, I am guilty of sexual immorality. And I take full responsibility for the entire problem." This came from a mega-pastor who has led millions of people astray; it's impressive, but hardly surprising.

Here is another shocker: we are working, eating, and sleeping with homosexual people and don't realize it. You'd be shocked at who is sleeping with whom. Your dad might be sleeping with your brother. "Oh," you might say, "they always play cards together." Open your eyes; don't be deceived. You just don't understand the depth and breadth of this problem.

No matter how you look at it or dress it up, it is wrong. In the book of Leviticus, the Bible tells us it is "an abomination before the Lord." Two men cannot reproduce. God wasn't thinking about Adam and Steve when He urged us to be fruitful and multiply. And the same is true for Eve and Eve. There are no lesbian or gay parties in Heaven, people! I would hate for any of my family members to marry a pastor who holds the conviction that same-sex marriage is acceptable.

These are the same pastors who seem to be away from the church all the time, praying for the sick and making home visits. Right! Be real with yourselves!

Some of these snakes are out there having oral sex and penetrating some church member's ass—could be the church cameraman, who is to say? Sad to say, we all may have gays and lesbians in our churches or our families.

Satan is trying to stop reproduction and God's Word. Homosexuality is a sin and God hates sin; as people of God, we are called to hate sin, as well. But remember…we are to love the sinner. I feel deeply that a person is not born gay; as I have said before, I sincerely believe it is a choice.

The Bible says, "What God made was good, and very good." So whether down-low or out of the closet, homosexuality is a sin, just as well as having sex outside of the marriage is a sin.

The only way to be delivered from sin is to ask the Lord God Almighty for forgiveness and to ask Him to deliver you from the bad things you are holding on to. We, as a people, seem to feel that we have no right to discriminate against anyone because our ancestors were persecuted. That's the wrong way of thinking. If you accept Christ, believe in Him and hold on to God's Word, you know that you *will* be persecuted. So it is written, so it certainly shall be done.

For lack of a better phrase, it is our cross, as Christians, to bear. Jesus Christ was sorely persecuted and crucified for delivering His message and for taking His stand. What makes you or I think we are above persecution? It pains me when people call themselves Christians and yet continue to live in blatant opposition to God's Word.

Do you truly believe you can be saved and yet behave any way you like? I guarantee you Bishop Long, Pastor Osteen, Pastor Dollar and Bishop Jakes can answer that question. Do you think you can ignore the truths of the Bible and still get that golden ticket to the pearly gates of Heaven? Apparently these mega-snakes do.

If you're a sinner all your life, yet while free falling from a plane at thirty thousand feet you suddenly repent and ask for God's forgiveness before you hit the ground, will you be saved? I don't dare question how the Lord would handle this particular situation...but I'm not going to try Him.

What does it mean to be saved? It is a lifestyle change...a gradual one. It's not an overnight thing. Examine yourselves to see if your faith is really genuine. Test yourselves. If you cannot tell that Jesus Christ is among you, it means you have failed the test.

No one has to live in the bondage of an abnormal life; not that of homosexuality or any other abnormal lifestyle. No one has to be controlled by pornography or alcohol or drugs. No one has to have evil thoughts plague their minds. There is a way out through what

Jesus has done for us. He loves sinners and wants to free us from evil practices. He will empower those who cry out for deliverance, those who long to be free and to stay free. Pray for deliverance.

Things aren't always as they seem. The Book of Proverbs warns that we can be deceived into believing we are going down the right path, yet be heading toward death, in the opposite direction from God's will. Don't forget the wages of sin, and do not assume every opportunity that arises comes from God. Satan will disguise himself.

The Holy Spirit will help you understand truth and experience an abundant life. Trust Him as He leads you. It's humorous how devout and Bible-savvy church folk make themselves out to be to blind sheep. They will memorize, quote and live every essence of "their Bible" to the end of their days, but fail to realize that the Bible they so adhere to and hold so close is not the true Word of God. The high rate of AIDS in our community is killing us and we are allowing those who agree with or condone immoral behavior to rewrite scripture to fit their views.

By its very nature, evil wants to silence or corrupt good. When good doesn't fight back, and allows evil to exist—at times taking the form of a corrupt pastor—exactly what spiritual war is being won? Be leery of people who say they are Christian, but ignore scripture; those who loudly condemn immoral acts but quickly point out that the Bible has been wrongly used in the past to spread hate and prejudice. Yes, it has happened...but only through lies and trickery.

I fear for us; we are becoming like them. We kill our souls, acting as though we are one with these misguided people. Brothers and sisters, this is serious business. We must take a stand. Not a stand in church, while the choir is yelping and Bishop Jakes looking up women's dresses. I mean a *real* stand, a stand led by our hearts, our minds and most of all, by our faith. And let us remember as we teach, we must also love and encourage.

To my homosexual brothers and sisters, I say there is a better way and that way is Jesus! Homosexuality is a sin. Lying is a sin. Adultery is a sin. All these behaviors are the result of choices we make. If you really do not want to be a homosexual, ask God to deliver you and He will. Homosexuality is a sin against God's Word, and such unions should not be allowed in a country established as "...one nation under God." Homosexuals should not be allowed to marry; instead we should encourage them to get right with God.

There is a stunning testimony about a gay man who did not receive the truth about sexual immorality. He lived his life based on false doctrine; doctrine force fed him by false prophets. On his deathbed, he accepted that the life he had lived as he chose brought consequences he could not change. Trusting a false prophet instead of God's Word concerning sexual immorality will lead you to disaster. Homosexuality, adultery, fornication, bisexuality — any sexual variation outside of the male-female covenant of marriage will subject you to its inherent dangers.

Added to bestiality, (Leviticus 18:23) homosexuality was one of the sins that resulted in God's giving the land of Canaan to the Israelites. The previous occupants were guilty of such sins (Leviticus 18:24-25). But the Israelites, too, were warned that if they engaged in the same kind of sins, they would also be "vomited out" of the land (Leviticus 18:23:30).

Homosexual conduct is an abomination unto the Lord.

"Put on the whole armour of God that ye may be able to stand against the wiles of the devil. For we wrestle not against flesh and blood, but against principalities, against powers, against the rulers of the darkness of this world, against spiritual wickedness in high places."

—Ephesians 6:11-12

THE BOOTY SHAKING PASTOR

CHAPTER 3
THE BOOTY SHAKING PASTOR

When it comes to booty shaking women, and hiding assets, the well-known Prosperity Pastor Rev. Dr. Dollar is no stranger. The Rev. Dr. Creflo Dollar has become something of a hip-hop icon. He appeared in a music video, "Welcome to Atlanta," by Jermaine Dupri and Ludacris. Pastor Dollar is one cool guy that's sending his followers straight to the pits of hell. Watch pastor Dollar booty shaking video at http://www.youtube.com/watch?v=kpkz1aWb_OE. If you are truly called to preach the word of God, you will not be involved with the devils work such as, worldly music, booty shaking or with women shaking their behinds.

Dollar has been involved in several controversial

events. Once, during the divorce of former heavyweight boxing champion Evander Holyfield, Dollar played a role in the hiding and transferring of Holyfield's assets before the divorce was filed. Police was about to arrest Dollar for contempt of court for refusing to give the court financial records in the divorce proceeding of former boxing champion Evander Holyfield and his wife Janice. Dollar, who has been leading his flock to the pits of hell, and claims he has prospered since following his teachings, members are required to tithe and show church leaders their personal financial information.

He is often videoed wearing a three-piece charcoal pinstriped suit as he preaches his message of prosperity as the hope of the gospel to his church.

He is the Pastor of World Changers Christian Center, riding in style in his two Rolls-Royces (which he continues to lie about telling his congregation that the second one was given to him—the church purchased the first one for him). He flies in a $5 million private jet to his speaking engagements in the United States and Europe. He lives in a $1 million dollar home behind iron gates in an upscale Atlanta neighborhood and owns another worth $1.27 million. Dollar is often accompanied by bodyguards in public. Remember, this is the pastor who appeared in a rap video, with Ludacris, while women shook their behinds. This is very impressive, but yet surprising for a man that is not teaching the true gospel (idol God). "Behold, you [idols] are nothing, and your work is nothing! The worshipper who chooses you is an abomination [extremely disgusting and shamefully vile in God's sight]," (Isaiah 41:24).

Mr. Creflo seemingly uses the acronym KISS (Keep It Simple and Stupid), and thousands of people say "Amen!"

It's actually fairly amazing how booty shaking Dollar can take literally any scripture from the Bible, and turn it into a sermon about why it is your God-appointed duty to give Mr. Dollar your money. And that God will then bless you, abundantly, with more money, so you can turn around and send that money to Mr. Dollar for his new $5 million dollar jet, and then you will be blessed with great wads of cash.

I must indeed say it's an attractive message, that God wants you to be rich, today, here on earth. That it is your duty to start raking in piles of cash. And you can trust the message, can't you? Because someone that God "anointed" is telling you to act on it, right? This is a man who openly claims to be "anointed." A man who claims he can pass his "anointing" on to you. A man who openly claims that the Biblical word "anointing" and the Biblical word "blessing" are one and the same thing! (Hint: he knows you're not going to look it up). "In their greed these teachers will exploit you with stories they have made up. Their condemnation has long been hanging over them, and their destruction has not been sleeping," (2 Peter 2:3 NIV).

Creflo Dollar repeats, constantly in his messages: "This is the Biblical formula on how to get rich!" Is it true? Is there a mathematical formula in the Bible that if you employ, it actually works? It has to work? There's no option but that it works? Mr. Dollar tells his swelling audience, "I could talk to you about spiritual things, but that's not what you need! You need to pay off your debts! You need to make money!" Send me your money, God will send you more money, and you can take half to pay off your debts, and send me the other half out of your appreciation — appreciation to me, the Sower, and appreciation to God Almighty, my boss. Jesus says: "Lay up your treasure in heaven," and Dollar retorts: "No! No! NO! Y'all need that money NOW!"

In one sermon, apropos of nothing, Mr. Dollar angrily shook his Bible at the congregation. "Why do I drive around in a Rolls Royce? Tell me that! Why do I own a big Rolls Royce? It's because God got some of you together; He had my congregation get together, and He told you to buy me a Rolls Royce, and you obeyed Him, you thought I deserved a Rolls Royce for what I teach you, and that's why I drive a Rolls Royce! I ain't ashamed of it!"

Very spiritual, wouldn't you agree? The Anointed Dollar preached on "The Parable of the Sower," which almost any preacher would correctly handle as either **a.)** The Gospel goes out and people receive it, and either bury it deep where it flourishes, or it ends up failing in one way or another, or **b.)** People choose God and later change their mind; those would be the two proper ways of handling this parable told by Jesus. But, to no surprise, the Anointed Dollar changed it into a "Prosperity" message, chiefly that Creflo Dollar is a "Sower" (instead of the Son of man, the True Anointed One), and he does this for a living, sowing seeds, so you need to give him his seeds so he can plant them in all kinds of interesting places, and then YOU will receive the bountiful harvest!

In other words, send Creflo Dollar your dollars, and you will be blessed by God. The Bible says "invest in treasures in heaven," but Creflo Dollar will teach you that it is bad translation, that in fact "God is gonna invest in YOU, right here, on earth!"

Jesus handled precisely this same twisted teaching in His parable of "The Rich Man and Lazarus." In this parable, Jesus has the rich man ending up in hell (whom the Pharisees considered BLESSED), whereas the poor Lazarus (cursed, the teachers taught) is blessed in heaven. Jesus was straightening out the Pharisees who believed exactly what Creflo Dollar teaches, that rich people are blessed, and poor people are cursed. It was a lie then, and it is a lie today. The "Anointing," and "Money," that is Creflo Dollar's version of "Gospel."

And Creflo Dollar, amazingly, regardless of his twisted theology and "creed of greed," is getting richer. Poor people are sending him their hard-earned dollars, hoping to get their formula blessed by God, hoping for some of Mr. Dollar's wealth and prosperity to fall on them.

Unfortunately, the poor are only getting poorer while Mr. Creflo Dollar gets wealthier and wealthier. But maybe THAT's the way God wants it to be? Dollar should employ his own formula. He should give $1 billion to all the followers he has scammed through the years, and he should repent of his greed. And perhaps God will bless him a hundredfold for his seed—imagine that, God will give Creflo Dollar $100 billion, and then he can, in turn, give that back to the people he has bilked, repenting, and then God will increase that seed a hundredfold (okay, already this has surpassed my meager math skills). Imagine if Dollar employed his own formula. There probably wouldn't be a poor person in America.

If you are one who has been tricked into sending him money or to his brothers in deceit, Bishop Eddie Long, Bishop T.D. Jakes and Joel Osteen, don't be angry, and don't blame it on God. Just learn from your mistake, warn others, and come more fully to God's true message of salvation, grace and deliverance. He wants you safely in His fold. Follow Him, not false men. Keep your eyes on Jesus, not on twisted shepherds who only want to fleece the sheep.

Just as booty shaking Creflo seems to confuse the nature of God, he also confuses the nature of man, which becomes crucial. He teaches we have equality and no inferiority to God in His righteousness and abilities on earth. But for one to get this understanding their mind needs to be renewed in the area of righteousness (like Pastor Dollar needs), so they can embrace the full truth of it by faith. Let's reference a scripture used by booty shaking Creflo that will just stun you.

Quoting John.10:34 and Psalms.82:6 Creflo states, "Wow. Let's read verse 6, ready read: 'I have said ye are gods and all of you are children of the most high. But you shall die like men and fall like one of the princes.' Well, we know who that is right? 'Arise oh God, judge the earth for thou shall inherit all the nations.' Now, notice what He says here, 'Ye are gods' small g. You are gods? Somebody says 'You trying to say we're gods?' No, I'm not trying to say we're gods. He already said it. But what I want to know is Lord, how can we be gods? And He answers it in the next phrase, 'Because you are the children of the Most High.' See if you are truly a child of God, if you were born out of God, you got to be a part of the God class.' I know I'm not God. But I'm a child of the Most High...I'm a part of the God class.... But then the next verse says, 'Because you did not believe you were gods, you're going to die like men.' But it says you're gods. And I said now, Lord, wait a minute here. How we going to prove this? Because I kept hearing over and over again all this week, we need to have a God training class for Christians. So they can start acting...," (sermon: "Our equality with God through righteousness 1/21/2001").

This is not what the next verse actually says, booty shaking Creflo who moves in and around the Scriptures at a fast pace makes it hard for anyone to check on these statements as he brings them through his twist and turns to his conclusions. (Psalms. 82:6-8) 'I said, 'You are gods, and all of you are children of the Most High. But you shall die like men, and fall like one of the princes.'

The Biblical application of this verse was addressed to the judges of Israel. They were called gods not because they were divine, but because they represented the true and only God when they judged the people. The word for God that is used here is elohim, which can mean rulers (not Yahweh Elohim used only for the one God). The word for judges is found in Ex.21:22; 22:8-9;

it is ha elohim (other scriptures of how the acted), (Deut.1:16; 16:18; 25:1 ;)(2 Sam.11:7). Jesus goes on to explain: They "will die as mere men and fall as one of the princes," that prince was Satan. They thought they were like God but they will die as mere men. It is then they will know the difference between the creator who is the true God and their own mortality. Juxtapose this with the end of Psalms.82 in verse 8: "Arise, O God, judge the earth; for You shall inherit all nations." It points to only one God who eventually will judge righteously and rule over all the people one day. Nowhere in Scripture is there a teaching of little gods verses big God, but instead the scripture teaches about false gods verses the true God. So in reality to claim to be a little god is to put one in the category of a false god.

To understand what Creflo teaches, we need to go back to the beginning, man's beginning in the garden and compare what he says happened in the Biblical account. Creflo has constructed a unique fairy tale from the Genesis record about Adam and God; from this distortion it affects almost everything else he believes; tithing, righteousness, Christ, healing, etc. In fact, it goes to the core difference on the nature of man and God. For it affects the concept of mans relationship to God—we being servants to Him as our King.

Although Creflo likes to see women shake their behinds, and like to have fun in worldly videos, he is leading his followers to the pits of hell. I see that churches focus largely around the minister and the personality of the minister. The size of the congregation becomes evident of the quality of the Christian commitment rather than the measure of concern and solidarity with the poor, weak and marginalized. It's not reality. It's entertainment. You should not care what pastor Dollar says, you should care what the Lord says.

It has been shown that Pastor Dollar is worshipping an Idol God; Pastor Dollar is a liar and a deceiver who is teaching his followers not the true gospel. Dollar does not care about saving a person's soul; he cares about getting rich and praying to his idol God that his followers hit the spiritual lottery. He preaches the same thing the rappers are saying "get rich or die trying." So that is why Creflo Dollar is with the booty popping women in the video "Welcome to Atlanta."

Until Pastor Dollar falls down on his knees and repent, nothing will change. He is still going to be ignorant. Creflo Dollar should not on the pedestal that people have perched him on.

I am not attacking any man who serves God. However, I am attacking those who are falsely preaching the Word of God. It is wrong to have men in the pulpit serving an Idol God. It is not only Pastor Dollar, but many preachers today are using the pulpit as a source of income. You just need to pray and have a personal relationship with God.

Here is a not-so-shocking letter I received about "Cashflo" Dollar.

Thank you so much for exposing this crook. I used to attend World Changer in 1992-93, prior to them moving into the dome they are in today. Creflo had me chasing material wealth like never before. I had always had the desire to be rich one day. A lady friend who ended up being my ex-wife introduced me to the church. To make a long story short, I paid my tithes and offerings and followed Creflo teachings faithfully without missing a service.

I found myself trying to be like Creflo instead of trying to be like Christ. I ended up in the mental institution. I literally lost my mind focusing on the material world instead of the spiritual world and the Kingdom of God. Creflo teaches prosperity without repentance from sin. Today I am delivered from this false teaching and I seek spiritual prosperity, the peace, love and joy of the Holy Spirit, the Kingdom of God. Today I can't even watch Creflo on television, his teachings are so off. He is definitely preaching another gospel aside from that of Jesus Christ. I'm sure I am not the only person who went into the mental institution following his doctrine of demons.

Tim, Atlanta, Georgia

"If anyone teaches false doctrines and does not agree to the sound instruction of our Lord Jesus Christ and to Godly teaching, he is conceited and understands nothing. He has an unhealthy interest in controversies and quarrels about words that result in envy, strife, malicious talk, evil suspicions and constant friction between men of corrupt minds, who have been robbed of the truth and who think that godliness is a means to financial gain.

But godliness with contentment is great gain. For we brought nothing into the world, and we can take nothing out of it. But if we have food and clothing, we will be content with that. People who want to get rich fall into temptation and a trap and into many foolish and harmful desires that plunge men into ruin and destruction. "For the love of money is a root of all kinds of evil. Some people, eager for money, have wandered from the faith and pierced themselves with many griefs,"

—1 Timothy 6:3-10

"TOUCH NOT MINE ANOINTED"

CHAPTER 4
"TOUCH NOT MINE ANOINTED"

God is about to do a great turnover that will involve leaders and ministries such as Eddie Long, Creflo Dollar, Joel Osteen and T.D. Jakes. Many people reading this book will immediately call to mind (Psalms 105:15), which says, "Touch not the Lord's anointed, and do my prophets no harm."

So that we can see what God is talking about here, let us quote the entire passage, starting with verse 10: "And confirmed the same unto Jacob for a law, and to Israel for an everlasting covenant, saying, Unto thee will I give the land of Canaan, the lot of your inheritance; When they were but a few men in number; yea, very few, and strangers in it. When they went from one nation to another, and from one kingdom to another people; He suffered no man to do them wrong; yea, he reproved kings for their sakes; Saying, Touch not mine anointed, and do my prophets no harm," (Psalms 105:10-15).

The immediate context of the verse is a reference to the patriarch Jacob. Just what kind of hazard was Jacob in fear of as he wandered from one nation to another people? Did he live in mortal dread that someone, somewhere, would criticize him? No, his concern was that the heathen would use physical violence against him. Read his complaint in (Genesis 34:30): "And Jacob said to Simeon and Levi, Ye have troubled me to make me to stink among the inhabitants of the land, among the Canaanites and the Perizzites: and I being few in number, they shall gather themselves against me, and slay me; and I shall be destroyed, I and my house."

It is clear that to touch the Lord's anointed is to commit an act of physical violence against the one anointed by God. It does not refer to those who verbally attack and criticize a preacher and his doctrine.

For further confirmation of this, see (I Samuel 24:6-7), where David had an opportunity to have King Saul killed, but refused to take advantage of it: "And he said unto his men, The Lord forbid that I should do this thing unto my master, the Lord's anointed, to stretch forth mine hand against him, seeing he is the anointed of the Lord. So David stayed his servants with these words, and suffered them not to rise against Saul. But Saul rose up out of the cave, and went on his way." Immediately afterward, David publicly criticized Saul in front of 3000 of Saul's troops, as well as his own 600 men, saying "The Lord judge between me and thee, and the Lord avenge me of thee: but mine hand shall not be upon thee. As sayeth the proverb of the ancients, Wickedness proceedeth from the wicked, but mine hand shall not be upon thee," (1 Samuel 24:12-13). No one seemed to feel that David was touching the Lord's anointed by this open rebuke of Saul. It is clear that to touch the Lord's anointed involved violence against his person, not criticism, rebuke or public disagreement.

Too many evangelists today use Bible threats such as "don't touch God's anointed." They claim the critics are speaking against a "man of God." Furthermore, if you are really anointed, you don't have to make threats. It is God who protects His anointed. Pastors and church leaders today who quote this verse don't mention what it is referring to.

The Bible has many passages that warn us to, carefully, evaluate church leaders. "He must hold firmly to the trustworthy message as it has been taught, so that he can encourage others by sound doctrine and refute those who oppose it," (Titus 1:9).

People spend hours and hours telling others not to

touch the so-called anointed, but they never take the time to open their Bibles to see if there is any validity to the demand. Many churchgoers just sit there and let their preacher guide them in the wrong direction.

It truly bothers me when I see church leaders act as if they have God's anointing and that people have to get it from them. How many times have believers been subjected to mishandled scriptures with an implicit or explicit "touch not God's anointed" if they dared to question the speaker? This is in contrast to the Biblical admonition to "try the spirits," (1 John 4:1).

Fear is not of God and teaching which incorporates psychological intimidation is corrupt and deceptive. One of the easiest ways to determine what "spirit" motivates a person in authority is to question them. A godly man or woman will never be offended or become indignant if someone dares to question them and compare what is said with the Word of God.

Many prominent pastors and evangelists today make the claim that because "souls" are being saved and "healings" take place in their church, their ministry is somehow validated. These things may be well and good, but they are no indication of divine sanction.

Jimmy Swaggart has been shown to be a whoremonger and Jim Bakker a thief, yet both of these saw thousands saved and miracles take place right in their own churches. Because one is blessed with "prosperity" and has a "following" of thousands, doesn't mean much when it comes to integrity and Godly sanction; for "He maketh his sun to rise on the evil and on the good, and sendeth rain on the just and on the unjust," (Matt. 5:45).

Anyone who tells you not to question a spiritual leader's teaching is someone you should avoid. Any spiritual leader who refuses to answer your questions about their doctrine is not the person you should be learning from. These are false teachers and will not only take your money...they will lead you straight to hell.

Today, Psalms 105:15 is often wrongly used, and amounts to nothing short of spiritual terrorism.

Let me remind you: a lie becomes the truth if it's spread long enough.

"For there shall arise false Christs, and false prophets, and shall shew great signs and wonders; insomuch that, if it were possible, they shall deceive the very elect."

—Matthew 24:24

THE FOUR TOP MEGA PIMPS

CHAPTER 5
THE FOUR TOP MEGA PIMPS

W hat is my reward then? Verily that, when I preach the gospel, I may make the gospel of Christ without charge, that I abuse not my power in the gospel," 1 Corinthians 9:18.

According to the Bible, Bishop Eddie Long, Bishop T.D. Jakes, Pastor Creflo Dollar and Pastor Joel Osteen are using the Word of God to manipulate true believers for fame and fortunes.

Let me start by saying these four pimps have made spiritual prostitution legal, and no one is doing anything about it. We are too deceived to realize what they have done, and continue to do.

The Encarta Dictionary defines prostitution as: *misuse of talent: the use of a skill or ability in a way that is considered unworthy, usually for financial gain.* There are more criminals in the pulpit than there are in jails. Christ made it clear that Satan would search us out. Pastors such as Pastor Dollar looks for our weaknesses and concentrates on that area of our lives. "And be not conformed to this world: but be ye transformed by the renewing of your mind, that ye may prove what is that good, and acceptable, and perfect, will of God," (Roman 12:2). As believers, we should not be conformed to worldly methods to teach Godly values.

Bishop Eddie Long, Pastor Joel Osteen, Pastor Creflo Dollar and Bishop T.D. Jakes have been lying to their church members, telling them the promises of God without teaching about His expectations of them. These pimps teach if you "sow a seed, God will richly bless you." These pastors are using the quantity of material goods as a means of measuring God's blessings in one's life. Here is another shocker, the majority of their churches are supported, for the most part, by the lower class—single heads of households—women who are living paycheck to paycheck.

Single women and supporters have to make decisions between using their monies to pay for prescriptions, feed their children or give money to the mega pimps and their royal families. Warn your friends and family to stay away from these four liars. They are watching over your checkbook, as well as your underage child. And, on that note, watch out for Bishop Eddie Long. They care nothing about your soul. Have you ever heard these pimps say God wants you debt free? Sure, and the reason they continue to feed you that phony line is so that you can have more money to give to them for their lifestyles. They are flaunting their million dollar homes, expensive cars, tailor-made suits and worldly materialistic goods, covering it with twisted scriptures so people will continue to give to their corporate empires. As they get richer, they won't even help with your grocery or gas bills. These four pimps care nothing at all about you, your family, or your souls. All they're concerned with is your checkbook. What's really scary is that people continue to fall for the twisted messages.

If they preach messages about any aspect of Christian discipline, rest assured it will end up with their pockets getting fatter and you worrying about how you're going to keep your electric from being disconnected or buy groceries for your family.

The Bible clearly tells us, "For what is a man profited, if he shall gain the whole world, and lose his own soul?" (Matthew 16:26). We fail to realize how serious and dangerous it is to be bound by these false prophets and their teachings. These four pimps prey on the weakest, dumbest, Americans, convincing people that they have a direct line to the Big Man, yet people send them money and tune in to their false teachings. Millions of dollars are being paid to see these pimps twist the Word of God.

Mega Fest, in Atlanta, was canceled by Bishop T.D. Jakes because there was not enough money being made to support his other ministries. How much do you suppose Jesus charged for His Sermon on the Mount? Bishop Jakes, and all the other pimps, broadcast on national television and tell the world that they have a life-changing book for you to buy. Don't get it twisted and do not fall under their spell; the Bible is the only life-changing book that I know of.

As a talk show host, I have heard stories of people who haven't eaten, have been evicted or lost their homes. Those families were tricked into giving a "seed offering," while Bishop Jakes, Pastor Dollar, Pastor Osteen and Bishop Long laughed all the way to the bank.

Eddie Long, wearing his tight muscle shirts, Creflo Dollar with his booty shaking women, and the other pimps on television can look right at the camera and, with a straight face, say, "The Lord is telling me that for you to have your breakthrough, you need to sow a seed of one thousand dollars or more." This is nothing less than spiritual prostitution. Nothing is being taught about Jesus redeeming people from their sins. Yet audiences

97

shout, lift up holy hands, fan their dresses in the air so that Pastor Osteen can be impressed, pay all their hard-earned money in tithes and offerings, and go home with a good feeling. Yet, these same people are still divorcing and remarrying, having sex with members of the church, cursing, indulging in homosexual activity, hitting the crack pipe, and more.

Take a hard look at how these pimps live and how they subsidize their lifestyles. According to Forbes.com, Bishop Eddie Long drives a $350,000 luxury car—that won't get him to heaven, nor can he take it to the grave—and lives in a $1.4 million six-bedroom, nine-bath mansion on twenty acres. Some people will not make that kind of money in a lifetime but this so-called man of God is tied up in materialistic, worldly possessions. I'm reminded that Jesus rode a humble donkey, and God used the jawbone of an ass.

Does He have a use for pimps such as Bishop Long, Pastor Dollar, Pastor Osteen or Bishop Jakes? Creflo—I call him "Cashflo"—has two Rolls-Royces. He lies to his congregation, telling them one was given to him, when in fact the church purchased the first one for him. He flies in a $5 million private jet to speaking engagements in the United States and Europe. His church also owns a Gates Lear Jet with an estimated value of $985,000. He lives in a million-dollar home behind iron gates, in an upscale Atlanta neighborhood, and owns another house worth $1.27 million. Like other world faith teachers, Dollar is often accompanied by bodyguards. Nowhere in the Bible can I find where Jesus employed an entire entourage of bodyguards to protect Him.

These four preach, "No weapon that is formed against thee shall prosper; and every tongue that shall rise against thee in judgment thou shalt condemn," (Isaiah 54:17). Is that a confusing message? Why do they need an entourage to protect them at church, in public and in the privacy of their homes? Because it's only a show; they strive to entertain their members and present themselves as they are not. Don't be misguided; these pimps are in it for the fame and fortune.

Bishop T.D. Jakes has moved west to a multi million-dollar, seventeen-acre estate in Fort Worth, Texas. According to Tarrant County records, The Jakes' new home has four bedrooms, five baths and a six-car garage.

The *New York Times* reported, in 2006, that Joel Osteen, pastor of Lakewood Church in Houston, Texas, could earn as much as $13 million on the contract he signed to write his second book. According to Nielsen Media Research, seven million Americans view Osteen's weekly sermons on television. That alone tells you how many good people are being deceived and condemned to the pits of hell. Just because "good ol' Joel Osteen" has a soft-spoken voice and weaves jokes into his sermons, doesn't mean he knows what he's talking about. Remember, he quit college to help his father's church grow. He's has no training for the ministry. He got his training from the Internet, just like all the others. Do the research yourself; you'll see.

Satan has many ways of showing up and using people like Pastor Joel Osteen. Osteen receives $200,000 in compensation from Lakewood Church, which recently leased the Compaq Center, former home of the NBA's Houston Rockets, to house his activities. He has a four-book deal and spends $12 million annually on television airtime.

We need to stop supporting and defending these pimps. We need to be defending the Word of God, which says, "For all men are like grass, and all their glory is like the flowers of the field; the grass withers and the flowers fall, but the Word of the Lord stands forever," (1 Peter 1:24-25).

Remember the money you spend when you have to impress the pastor, trying to make it appear as if you care about him; or when it's time for the pastor's anniversary, for his speaking engagements, for a "mega-fest," a cruise, or to buy his books? What really concerns me is that so many followers are so confused that the ringing of a cash register sounds the same to them as the ringing of a church bell.

These four pimps, and all the other prosperity liars, are all about your money. If you really study Creflo Dollar's messages, you will note that he plays on the carnal weakness of the spiritually-blind humans who desire prosperity. They teach people to trust in giving money for blessings while they use the Word of God as their tool. Carnal-minded people can't see that these pimps are rich only because other carnal people send a lot of money in, with the misguided hope of hitting the spiritual lottery. We need to trust in Jesus not these preachers of darkness. "But seek first the kingdom of God and His righteous, and all these things shall be added to you," (Matthew 6:33). These pimps are not teaching about seeking the Kingdom of God or seeking God's righteousness; they are teaching how a person can have an abundance of worldly things, and reinforcing the all-too-human failing of greed.

This is wrong, very wrong. I know God is not pleased with Bishop Eddie Long, Bishop T.D. Jakes, Pastor Joel Osteen and Pastor Creflo Dollar. I'm encouraging everyone; don't be deceived by these four pimps who will lead you straight down the road to hell. Jesus came to seek and to save those who are lost, and these pimps don't see people as lost. They see them as spiritually and emotionally desperate marks, who can be fleeced with a superficial assurance of God's blessing.

Bishop Eddie Long, Pastor Creflo Dollar, Pastor Joel Osteen and Bishop T.D. Jakes have entered into what they call "ministries," merely to fulfill their own personal desires, not because they were called to fulfill God's purpose of preaching the gospel to every living creature.

These four pimps have created their own species of religion that goes along with Christianity just enough to look appealing to the average person. They twist the scriptures, reciting the part of the verse that they want people to hear, taking the scriptures out of context.

They are brazen enough to stand in the pulpit and tell you, "Go and read it for yourself, don't believe me…," knowing that most people trust them and aren't going to take the time to check the references. But it pays to go back to the Bible, to read it carefully and get the real deal. Like newborns, we are so use to being fed to the point that when someone raises a challenge, and wants to hold these pimps accountable, we get uncomfortable. We become defensive and start calling these brave souls "haters."

The fact is that people of these mega-churches no longer open the Bible for themselves. They take what these pimps are preaching as "gospel." These pimps have misled millions and prostituted billions of dollars from believers and unbelievers alike by twisting the Word of God and using it for their personal gain.

The problem is that we, as the body of Christ, have gotten so comfortable with whatever these pimps give us that we're losing the ability to think for ourselves. These pimps use whatever is popular, or topical, for the sake of achieving their goals. They do not tell the truth from the pulpit because they don't want to step on the toes of the money givers. People love to hear about what God is going to do for their abundant life, but don't want to hear about saving their souls. Let us re-read 2 Timothy (2:14-19), "Keep reminding them of these things. Warn them before God against quarreling about words; it is of no value, and only ruins those who listen. Do your best to present yourself to God as one approved, a workman who does not need to be ashamed and who correctly handles the word of truth. Avoid godless chatter, because those who indulge in it will become more and more ungodly. Their teaching will spread like gangrene. Among them are Hymenaeus and Philetus, who have wandered away from the truth. They say that the resurrection has already taken place, and they destroy the faith of some. Nevertheless, God's solid foundation stands firm, sealed with this inscription: "The Lord knows those who are his," and, "Everyone who confesses the name of the Lord must turn away from wickedness."

There you will find the assurance that God's solid foundation stands firm, sealed with this inscription: "The Lord knows those who are His" and "Everyone who confesses the name of the Lord must turn away from wickedness."

Compare what is happening today with what Jesus and the apostles did. What passes for religion today is an exercise in men taking your money in order to enlarge themselves and their holdings. What they give in charity is sometimes not even ten percent of what they take in, but they demand at least ten percent in every tithing swindle.

Jesus said His followers should give to the poor. However, there is not one mega-church pimp who is poor. Give them nothing. The bills they claim they need to pay are the result of financial burdens related to material things, their ministries and the go-pleasing practice of seeing themselves on television, none of which is of help to the poor. That's what these pimps do. They want you to be generous to them, so they tell you things you want to hear. None of it is about the truth and upholding the true message of Jesus Christ. Ask, Joel Osteen; he will smile you right to the pits of hell and laugh all the way to the bank.

We treat these so-called men as if they are God: church members go to their homes to wash their cars, keep their children, mow the lawn, and cook their meals. Get a clue, Body of Christ! You are serving a *man*. You are putting all your trust in *man*. Even though, Psalms 56:11 clearly tell us, "In God have I put my trust: I will not be afraid what man can do unto me."

Jeremiah 14:14 says, "Then the LORD said unto me, the prophets are prophesying lies in my name: I sent them not, neither have I commanded them, neither spake unto them: they prophesy unto you a false vision and divination, and a thing of nought, and the deceits of their heart." The first false prophets were among the people of Israel. God is saying that He never commanded them, nor did He speak unto them. Yet in their bold defiance of truth, they began to teach out of their personal repositories of evil.

We are further cautioned in Jeremiah. 23:32, "Behold, I am against them that prophesy false dreams, saith the LORD, and do tell them, and cause my people to err by their lies, and by their lightness; yet I sent them not, nor commanded them: therefore they shall not profit this people at all, saith the LORD."

God is making a very clear declaration that He is against Bishop Eddie Long, Pastor Creflo Dollar, Pastor Joel Osteen and Bishop T.D. Jakes the false prophets who cause His people to stray. He warns His people that they will not prosper if they embrace the false teachings spewed forth from the mouths of false prophets.

"And many false prophets shall rise, and shall deceive many," (Mat 24:11). There will not be one specific false prophet; there will be many who are going to attack the Lord's sheep and try to deceive them. And, there are false prophets, both inside and outside, the church. Inside are the charismatic movement, dead orthodoxy, homosexuals in the pulpits and more; outside are the cults, the radio and television preachers with their political and watered-down ecumenical gospel.

Jesus warned us that there would be many false prophets such as Bishop Eddie Long, Pastor Creflo Dollar, Pastor Joel Osteen and Bishop T.D. Jakes, who will try to draw the people away from Him. In the same chapter, Jesus warns His children to flee to the Kingdom of God when we see such works of Satan. In our churches, these works must be considered the abomination of desolation, and the work of Satan. Satan is not omnipresent, so he cannot be in all the false churches at once—but his deceitful works can be seen in many places simultaneously.

Take a self-examination; be certain that you are worshiping God for who He is...not for what He can do for you.

"But there were false prophets also among the people, even as there shall be false teachers among you, who privily shall bring in damnable heresies, even denying the Lord that bought them, and bring upon themselves swift destruction."

— 2 Peter 2:1

BEWARE OF FALSE PROPHETS

CHAPTER 6
BEWARE OF FALSE PROPHETS

The word of God says, "Beware of the false prophets, who come to you in sheep's clothing, but inwardly are ravenous wolves. You will know them by their fruits. Grapes are not gathered from thorn bushes, nor figs from thistles, are they? Even so, every good tree bears good fruit; but the bad tree bears bad fruit. A good tree cannot produce bad fruit, nor can a bad tree produce good fruit. Every tree that does not bear good fruit is cut down and thrown into the fire. So then, you will know them by their fruits," (Matthew 7:15-20).

Sadly, Christians are falling into the traps of Satan through their trust of wealthy, prominent, religious men and women who no longer preach Jesus Christ or the

Bible. In these last days, many Christians have not had their mind renewed through the Word of God. They have not been sanctified through the washing of the blood of Jesus. Their faith centers on Christian icons instead of Jesus Christ and His purpose of giving them salvation to enter into His Kingdom.

So many in the Christian church have become cold and lukewarm, and they have given their minds over to forms of *Better Homes and Garden* and Disney World Christianity, lifestyles that are just seeking after material things and emotional experiences. Jesus is rarely preached, (Roman. 10:17), "So then faith cometh by hearing, and hearing by the word of God."

Are you listening to preaching that consists of stories about the minister, his or her family experiences; are you giving to them so that you can get some money to increase your depleted bank account?

Many of these preachers are living sumptuously like kings and queens in multi-million dollar homes while you sit overwhelmed by debt. I'm telling you that you are NOT listening to the real gospel. Repent for seeking after God the Father as a sugar daddy instead of the God that sent His Divine Son Jesus to save you from your sins, to give you eternal life. Rededicate your life to Jesus and ask Him where you can go to receive the true Gospel.

The Bible warns, "And be not conformed to this world: but be ye transformed by the renewing of your mind, that ye may prove what [is] that good, and acceptable, and perfect, will of God," (Roman. 12:2).

The New Age movement is the most deceptive and damaging philosophy around today. It is entwined not only in witchcraft and Satanism, but it is prevalent in all denominations of what the world calls Christianity. What most people do not understand is this is the same thing Satan said in the Garden of Eden to Eve. "You will be as Gods," (Genesis 3:4, 5). No one is a god but Jesus Christ. To accept yourself as a god puts you on the list of those going to hell.

Why is God silent in the face of widespread heresy? Why do the wicked seem to prosper while many godly are financially oppressed? When is God going to step on the scene and set it all right? We must take heart, though it may appear that God's enemies are in control and He is doing nothing, that it's just not true. God is waiting for the time when people will come to the understanding that apart from Him, they can do nothing. We must take heart to remember these times were foretold in the scriptures. God is in control and everything must be fulfilled. As the children in the wilderness were led by the hand of God, we shall see the majestic glory of the risen Lord!

God desires people who will trust Him and His

Word. When men cast aside God's laws, they do what is right in their own eyes. Despite how ungodly the world becomes, His people will see His deliverance! People's will for rebellion will continue until his demonic leaders bring the world to the brink of utter destruction. Christians may have to spend time in God's waiting room, having faith in Jesus, abiding, and contending with the wiles of Satan until the day of deliverance, but it will surely come.

Many famous preachers have changed their teachings to deny that Jesus Christ is Lord. Churches are undergoing radically restructuring of doctrine, structure, methods and practices and the reality of Jesus Christ and His Word.

1. False teachers are proud. They are concerned for their own popularity. They are concerned for their own fame. They are concerned for their own notoriety. They are concerned for their own prestige. They're concerned to see themselves and hear themselves in the public eye. They want large crowds, as it were, to bow down in great homage to them. They're characterized by pride and they will do anything to gain the ground they need to gain for the welfare of their own personal ego, including any amount of necessary compromise.

2. Secondly, False teachers are characterized by self-ishness. They tend to be self-centered. They are concerned for their own comfort. They are concerned for their own popularity. They are concerned for their own prosperity. In the end, it's all about money, fame, and prestige and notoriety, equaling an increased bank account. They are in it for the money and the personal material benefits that they can gain as they endeavor to feed their selfish desires.

3. Thirdly, They are characterized by deception. They usually can weave a very sophisticated web of deception in their teaching because they tend to be articulate, if they're going to be successful, and they endeavor to engage other people to aid them in their deceitful enterprise, which gives it the facade of credibility.

4. They're not only proud, selfish and deceptive, but they're irreverent. If there's anything that sort of dominates in my thinking about false teachers, it is their irreverence. They have absolutely no regard for God. The fact that they would go against God, and elevate themselves the way they do, and pervert the truth, indicates their utter irreverence. They have little, if any, regard for God, His Word, His truth, His glory, His honor.

5. Finally, they are spiritually destructive. They seek to use and abuse people, leading them into error, which destroys them, and into sin, which pollutes them.

Therefore, as you look at false teachers with regards to the world, they are proud and they seek fame and popularity. With regards to themselves, they are self-centered, self-aggrandizing, and self-gratifying. With their ministries, they are dishonest, deceptive and lack integrity. With regards to God, they are utterly irreverent; in fact, they are blasphemous. And, for the people they influence, they are spiritually destructive. Therefore, their relationship to the world, their ministries, to themselves, to God, and to their people all reflects the deviation of their hearts.

While many Christians slumber, there is intense suffering in the entire world. We need to wake up and "stand in the gap" and cry aloud and clear that there is only one . . . Jesus Christ! Christians should be filling in the void by telling the seeking world the answer is Jesus Christ.

"But there were false prophets also among the people, even as there shall be false teachers among you, who privily shall bring in damnable heresies, even denying the Lord that bought them, and bring upon themselves swift destruction. And many shall follow their pernicious ways; by reason of whom the way of truth shall be evil spoken of. And through covetousness shall they with feigned words make merchandise of you: whose judgment now of a long time lingereth not, and their damnation slumbereth not," (2 Peter. 2:1-3).

The Apostle warned, "But, there were false prophets also among the people, even as there shall be false teachers among you, who privily (craftily) shall bring in damnable heresies, even denying the Lord that bought them, and brings upon them themselves swift destruction. And many shall follow their pernicious (corrupting) ways; by reason of whom the way of truth shall be evil spoken of," (2 Peter. 2:1-1).

This warning is very clear. False teachers will arise who craftily teach heresies, which will deny the Biblical view of Jesus. Furthermore, according to a prophecy, many will believe these errors and follow them just as we see it happenings in our day! The charm and inspiration of pantheism have begun to exert its influence on the Church through unorthodox religious teachers. It has happened so subtly that few people have noticed.

As I look around the world of religion in our society, one thing has become very clear. The masks of the false shepherds of the apostate church are coming off. More and more, the false prophets of today's religious establishment are showing themselves to be the wolves in sheep's clothing. In years past, it has taken great discernment to see and hear the little bits of leaven they have used to poison their flocks. However, lately it seems the apostasy is much more open.

The most blatant examples are Pastor Joel Osteen and Bishop T.D. Jakes. Both were recently given an opportunity to proclaim the gospel on the national stage.

Osteen, in fact, was given that opportunity twice, once on the Larry King Show and again on the ABC daytime show, The View. Jakes had his chance during a lengthy interview on National Public Radio. Both were asked during the course of the interview if they believed that Jesus was the only way to heaven. Neither would say that Jesus is the way, the truth, and the life, and that no man comes to God except by him. Both of these wolves in sheep's clothing left room for some to come to God another way.

"Jesus saith unto him, I am the way, the truth, and the life: no man cometh unto the Father, but by me," (John. 14:6).

Several years ago, there was a story written about a man who deceived millions of people. This so-called *man of God* knew how to inspire hope. He was committed to people in need. He counseled prisoners and juvenile delinquents, started a job placement center, opened rest homes and domiciles for the retarded, had a health clinic, organized a vocational training center, provided free legal aid, founded a community center, preached about God, and he even claimed to cast out demons, perform miracles and heal.

There is no doubt in my mind that if someone looked at this ministry, they would have concluded that he was a true minister of God. The truth of the matter is that countless church leaders, governors, senators, congressional representatives, and even the President of the United States, recognized him for the great work he did. Little did they know he was no good.

Let us not evaluate things based on appearances; we will make a serious mistake. We may be in danger of being deceived and head for destructions. Remember Jesus said that, in the end, these false prophets would show great signs and wonders, so as to mislead, if possible. If we were to look at the outward manifestation of supernatural powers, we might be deceived. Satan is a supernatural being too. My brothers and sisters in Christ, we are living in these times today.

Jesus said that these false prophets would come to you in sheep's clothing. Take a moment and think about it. The perfect disguise for a dog seeking to have a lamb chop for dinner would be a sheep's suit. He might look like a dog and he may even smell like a dog, but on the inside, he would still be a hungry, vicious animal. That old saying, "If it walks like a duck and quacks like a duck, it is probably a duck," is not necessarily true. I must indeed say, we all walk and quack like many things that we are not. Wouldn't you agree?

The strategy that Satan uses is to appear to be something he is not. Do you think Satan will show up in a red suit and horns, pointed tail, and a pitchfork? Of course not; he would be exposed if he did.

We, as a people, need to examine the sound doctrine. We are exhorted in the Scriptures to give attention to sound doctrine, or proper scriptural teaching. A false prophet will give scriptures in a slightly twisted way in order to serve his own ends. That is why it is so important for us to get into the Bible for ourselves and have a personal relationship with God, in order not to be deceived by those.

Those who continue to be in deception, arrogance and fail to recognize their sin, the words are very clear. Do not receive him into your house, church, social group. This will only bring a curse into your lives and to the lives of others. It is important to note to break all ties and spiritual links with these types of people, and move on.

I close with this thought: have faith in God and not man. The Bible says that we are to live just as we received Christ as our Savior, by faith. The Bible also says that it is impossible to please God without faith. What is faith? Faith simply believes the Word of God and not the word of man. You were saved by believing and trusting God's promise of salvation through Jesus Christ. As you learn things from studying the Bible, God wants you to trust Him and apply what you learn to your life. In other words, trust and obey His command.

"And they come to Jerusalem: and Jesus went into the Temple, and began to cast out them that sold and bought in the Temple, and overthrew the tables of the moneychangers, and the seats of them that sold doves; And would not suffer that any man should carry any vessel through the Temple. And He taught, saying unto them, Is it not written, My House shall be called of all nations the house of prayer? But ye have made it a den of thieves. And the scribes and chief priests heard it, and sought how they might destroy Him: for they feared Him, because all the people was astonished at His doctrine."

—Mark 11:15-18

JEZEBEL JUANITA BYNUM

CHAPTER 7
JEZEBEL JUANITA BYNUM

Everybody knows Evangelist Juanita Bynum is a False prophetess. A wise woman once said, "remember how you got your man: that's the same way you are going to lose him."

The body of Christ needs no more silly drama played out before the world. Currently, things are just getting out of hand. We are seeing the end of all things. The false prophets and the prophetess such as Jezebel Bynum, Bishop Long, Bishop Jakes, Pastor Osteen and Pastor Dollar are being exposed for who they really are, "a liar and a deceiver". We the people are so foolish to follow these liars. Why are people ready to follow these liars? The Bible states in Second Timothy 4:3, "For the time will come when they will not endure sound doctrine; but after their own lusts shall they heap to themselves teachers, having itching ears."

What am I talking about? I'm talking about false Prophetess Juanita Bynum and her circus which have so many true believers fooled that it is ridiculous. Bynum has spread her witchcraft all over the body of Christ and has used her Jezebel anointing to conjure up a demonic influence that put her on every major platform of our so-called churches. She has bewildered the effeminate Bishops and manipulated the minds of silly women and men in order to elevate herself to a level which will not be challenged by any of the so called "leaders" of the body of Christ. But I, Reuben Armstrong, have got news for you. Those that lead her don't lead me! Those that are bewildered and under her Jezebel spell don't speak for me. I believe in the Bible and I believe in Jesus. I don't submit to Jezebel and I will never allow her witchcraft to put me under. But there are so many who have made Bynum their God.

First, this woman confesses her sins before everyone and goes in depth to describe her sexual appetite and her carnal craving in her message "No More Sheets." She then states that God does not allow her to wear makeup, pants, or any kind of outfits that will show her figure because her ungodly ways would rise up.

She basically began preaching in a choir robe with

a small Afro, free of weave, perms, curls, and gel. As the money poured in, her look began to change. But did any of the silly women who followed her and her, false god she serves, question her? "NO!" You don't question the prophetess, as she stated on TBN. Juanita Bynum said and I quote, "Don't you know you are all just a bunch of dumb sheep's?". Those were her exact words, not mine. I would never call the people of God dumb sheep's.

She began calling out T.D. Jakes and traveling around preaching against him. Once she saw that Bishop Jakes was able to shut down her engagements with his "power over-weak minded selfish pastors", she came to him and repented by handing him her shoes. After he laid hands on her and said "Daughter, thy sins are forgiven thee", she was back on the money trail. I didn't know we had the power to forgive sin like Christ, but I guess if we get enough money, folks will believe anything. She began hosting TBN and got her clearance from the Christian Mafia to travel around and rob people of their hard earned money.

There was another level that Jezebel needed to rise to and that was to destroy God's plan for success in marriage. Even though she had a failed marriage and Thomas Weeks was currently (at that time) in a marriage, the two had to come together to make this happen. So, they got married and had a million dollar wedding that they sold and marketed.

By now, her mixed audience had finally turned all black, as they always do. Single black women and women that are married to weak men began to flock to this Jezebel. She worked her magic to build a multi-million dollar empire. That's still not enough for Jezebel Bynum. Jezebel Juanita Bynum has to destroy the prophets of God, remember? She has to raise above the authority of men so she can lead.

The marriage conferences started after the first year of that farce of a marriage. I remember the first conference they had. My staff and I even tried to contact them about it because I couldn't understand how they had Bishop Noel Jones as the keynote speaker (who is divorced) and Tonex as the psalmist (who is divorced). I just couldn't understand why so many folks were following her. But they began to bankroll these conferences and fill the auditoriums as they discussed private, lewd behaviors that they shared together.

I remember Thomas Weeks saying that he loves it when Juanita uses dirty, cuss words during sex! And Juanita stated on several occasions that she would get mad and throw bricks at his car and objects at him. Juanita Bynum said that she really needed anger management when dealing with him. All of this was playing before the world like a dirty soap opera. But I assure you, it is the spirit of the Jezebel!

Jezebel Juanita had been planning all along to build confidence in marriage and then destroy all hope for a successful marriage. God said that marriage was a "good thing" so the Jezebel spirit had to prove God wrong and make marriages between so-called believers look hopeless. Understand that I do not condone men striking women under any circumstances. I understand from several sources that have witnessed the fights and brawls of the Weeks that this is not the first time they have had a physical altercation. She even admitted to using foul language in bed, so I'm sure she knew how to work those words to get this man to attack her. I'm not saying he should have knocked the hell out of her, but I am saying that this was all the plan of the Jezebel. Now Bynum can accomplish three feats with one shot. Since this man attacked her, she can now do what she wanted in the beginning. Here are the three things:

1. She can end that lie of a marriage that so many folks bought into. No one will question her and everybody will sympathize with her when she ends it. Even those that bought the video will forgive and forget because she was being abused. Now, she has the right to leave, right? If she is a true prophetess, wouldn't she know this was not the man to marry? If she took the vows to stay with him and she is the all-powerful prayer warrior she claims to be, can't she just pray this thing back into shape? Remember, the marriage was over before this fight. Why did she post the pictures of her bruises on her own myspace page the day after? Who shows their bruises to the world after a private altercation? "Juanita Bynum does that's who."

2. She can now capitalize on those bruises. She can hold conferences for battered women. I can just imagine her on the major talk shows such as Oprah, Tyra, Larry King and The Reuben Armstrong Show. Those little bruises are worth millions when you are in the business of exploiting personal issues for gain. Get ready for Juanita Bynum to cash in millions of dollars from books sold on battered women. Forget the marriage stuff, because a battered woman is worth more money than simply ending a marriage. Most of her followers are single and hurt black women, so this plays right into Juanita Bynum's hands. Get ready for the conference, "What's Love Got to Do with It Part II." that will eventually be a movie starring the prophetess, Juanita Bynum.

3. The so-called Bishop that beat her is toast! The man is made to look like the enemy and the woman is, of course, the victim. I'm not saying he shouldn't look bad, but I'm saying that his side of the story will mean nothing. The silly and lost women that follow this Jezebel don't want to hear the truth. The man will be made to look weak and crazy while the Jezebel's influence does what it always does by destroying the credibility of men and undermining the authority of men. Jezebel is controlling this situation and it's a shame. But the Bible warns us of this day coming and yet so many will ignore what the Word says for the sake of feeling better about their situations. They follow these junk ministries to make themselves feel better about the place they are in and the bad decisions they have made in life. So, they turn to fables and storytelling ministries that make them feel better just the way they are, without changing! The Bible says it like this: 2 Timothy 3:5 "They'll make a show of religion, but behind the scenes they're animals. Stay clear of these people." These are the kind of people who smooth-talk themselves into the homes of unstable and needy women and take advantage of them; women who is depressed by their sinfulness take up with every new religious fad that calls itself "truth." They get exploited every time and never really learn.

People of God, it is time to pray. Pray that this Jezebel spirit will be exposed for what it really is and that those who are blinded are granted site by the truth of the Word of God. Pray that these sorts of people are sat down and no longer allowed to flourish in the body of Christ and that the true remnant of God be revealed and lifted up before the world. We have totally forgotten that the world is watching this. These marriages are being abandoned and these false leaders are being lifted up to show the world hopelessness and perversion in the house of God. And the very ones we should be reaching are last on our list and now we are occupied by chasing these false prophets and prophetesses as they chase Hollywood, Fame, and Money! What about the sinners? What about the people who are on their way to hell? Why are we following Jezebel into the limelight? We should be following the Word and calling out the evil of Jezebel and her agenda, but an effeminate man and a silly woman will never do that because they need Jezebel to validate their own selfish ambitions.

Pray saints for the hour of Christ's return. If these events don't alarm you enough to make you see that His return is eminent, then I don't know what can get your attention. Pray that this whole drama gets reversed and Jezebel loses. Pray That the Weeks can reconcile and these marriages can be God centered and not self centered. Let's hope that they seek counsel and not pretend to be marital counselors anymore. Pray that I am wrong about the outcome of this and Juanita sees the error of her ways and Thomas Weeks repents and turns to God. We must pray because this ordeal is playing out to truly be Juanita Bynum's, the Jezebel, finest hour.

"Jesus answered: 'Watch out that no one deceives you. For many will come in my name, claiming, "I am the Christ," and will deceive many.'"

—Matthew 24:4-5

KNOW WHO YOU ARE

CHAPTER 8
KNOW WHO YOU ARE

B e ye not conformed to this world, but be ye transformed by the renewing of your mind, that ye may prove what is that good, and acceptable, and perfect, will of God," (Roman 12:2). This should say it all. As believers, we should not conform to worldly methods to teach Godly values. That is in itself a compromise of who we are. Bishop T.D. Jakes, Bishop Eddie Long, Pastor Joel Osteen and Pastor Creflo Dollar ought to stop lying to people, telling them of God's promises without preaching about His expectations of us. They would have us think we can get something for nothing.

Do you ever go to church and see people shouting and running all over the place? You sit and wonder if they're praising God or man. Sad to say, many people worship man more than they worship God. Some people will not come to church unless the pastor is there. If the Word of God is being taught according to the Bible, regardless of who's teaching it, why wouldn't you come to church, shout and kick those skirts up in the air? Because it's nothing but a show; it's acting.

One of my pet peeves is seeing people misled and taken by so-called "church leadership." Having been a victim of this, I know first hand how you can be lead astray in a subtle way that can alter the course of your life. Jesus teaches us in (Matthew 15:14), "If the blind lead the blind, they both fall into a ditch."

My challenge to churchgoers around the world is to be absolutely sure that God has called you to the church you attend. Good preaching and singing is not enough. Let the true spirit of God draw you there. Do not believe the hype to find out later that Bishop T.D. Jakes, Pastor Creflo Dollar, Pastor Joel Osteen, Bishop Eddie Long, or your church leader has mastered the art of preaching to you, while needing someone to preach to him.

In over thirty years of church experience, I have heard every excuse possible when a preacher is exposed for unrighteous living. And while God is the one who ultimately exposes, He will never expose anyone without first convicting and challenging the person to get it right. And it's important to understand that a person can function in his or her gift or calling without the anointing. Bishop Long, Bishop Jakes, Pastor Dollar and Pastor Osteen are doing it. God gives gifts He will never take back, but He will withdraw His anointing. Preaching is powerless without the anointing.

Here's a popular excuse: everyone sins. The Psalmsist David sinned and God still called him a man after His heart. True, but there were consequences for David's sin. He still functioned as the mighty man of war, he was still a gifted Psalmsist, but his sin cost him the building of God's temple. Look at Saul, whose throne David inherited. Saul was actually functioning as king while David was being anointed as king because of Saul's own sin. "But he that knew not, and did commit things worthy of stripes, shall be beaten with few stripes. For unto whomsoever much is given, of him shall be much required: and to whom men have committed much, of him they will ask the more," (Luke 12:48). The moral of this scripture is simply this: to whom much is given, much is required.

Today's church is impotent, partly because the anointing flows from the head down. When church leaders function but have no power, they lead a powerless people.

The devil knows that if he is able to get to the shepherd, the sheep will be lost and confused. "Awake, O sword, against my shepherd, and against the man that is my fellow, saith the Lord of hosts: smite the shepherd, and the sheep shall be scattered: and I will turn mine hand upon the little ones," (Zechariah 13:7).

"Then saith Jesus unto them, All ye shall be offended because of me this night: for it is written, I will smite the shepherd, and the sheep of the flock shall be scattered abroad," (Matthew 26:31).

Understand this, it is incumbent upon the shepherd to live above reproach, to practice what they preach, and to be more concerned about holiness than hype. With world events going as they are, we need pastors and shepherds who have the heart of God and will not mess with their sheep.

In the Bible, the Apostle Paul tells us he was in need of preaching to himself before he preached to others, lest he become unfit or a counterfeit. Unrighteousness in the head will produce unrighteousness throughout the body. In fact, there is so much more required of a pastor, I believe God will actually judge them more severely. I believe that it is possible to walk in the fivefold ministry gift of the pastor and be one hundred percent free from scandal and unrighteousness. God is awesome! He can take the mess in our lives and cause it to become our message. God can take our mistakes, our failures and even our secular means to bring glory to Himself.

This is why it is absolutely important for us to watch what we say. Guard your heart; out of it flows the issues of life. The key is that we must learn to guard our tongue because our words become our thoughts and our thoughts become our actions. Everything we do can be traced back to what we say and what we think.

In Matthew 16, Jesus was having a conversation with His disciples and He asked them a challenging question. He asked, "Who do men say that I am?" With everything that was being said about Jesus, He was trying to see if the men He trained had a revelation of who He was. Sometimes people who are supposed to be close to you don't really know who you are. Sometimes our circumstances try to define who we are. A person with little money may say "I'm poor." The abused child may say "I'm scared."

While it's easy to succumb to the labels of our circumstances and other people place on us, we must understand that we were predestined as God's royal ambassadors. He allowed us to come to the earth filled with purpose and potential. 1-Peter 2:9 says, "But that we are a chosen generation, a royal priesthood, an holy nation, a peculiar people; that ye should shew forth the praises of him who hath called you out of darkness in his marvelous light." We have been created with greatness and royalty. The devil has created havoc for some of us because he wants us to settle in, to camp out at a place where God never designed us to be.

In the garden, Satan enticed Eve by getting her to deny she was who God created her to be. While he was successful in that instance, just as he has been at times in all our lives, if we begin to talk ourselves out of our mess by saying the right things, we will see different results. When you begin to declare that you are a king—regardless of your gender or current challenge—your mind will change. Tell yourself that you won't settle for substandard living. You will not keep reliving your past mistakes. You will grind and stretch your faith because God made you to be a king.

We could very easily become what people call us. Instead, we should tap into what God calls us. One of the Bible's best-known characters is David. There was a time when David was frustrated. In addition to dealing with his own sin, someone was looking to kill him. Instead of giving up, he encouraged himself in the Lord. Instead of saying, "I'm going to die when Saul catches me," he encouraged himself. His circumstances changed because he saw himself as God saw him. I, myself, have known times when I wanted to say, "I quit." But by God's grace, I found the strength to say, "I won't quit. I'm a king."

When a king declares something, it becomes a fact.

If a king says you are going to die on Wednesday, make your arrangements; you are as good as dead. As kings and priests created by the King of Kings, we have the power to *declare* and see our declarations come to pass.

It's not what the enemy, your circumstances or other people call you, it's what you answer to that matters. Start answering by saying, "I'm a king" and watch how things change.

Every God-given principle for man's success has been perverted or misunderstood in some form or another. Understand that there is *creative power* in the words you speak. During the creation of man, God breathed the breath of life into man. The literal translation says, "...man became a speaking species like God." The same *creative power* that caused an earth that was without form to become the beautiful planet we now enjoy lives within us all. In Genesis, God spoke, and it *became*. According to Proverbs 18:21, "Death and life are in the power of your tongue: and they that love it shall eat the fruit thereof."

While the Word has the power to alter your outlook, true creative power comes when the Word of God is spoken out of your mouth. You don't have to be a theologian or a Bible scholar. All you have to do is find a scripture that expressed your desire and begin saying it or confessing it. When you first begin saying it or confessing it, your circumstances are out of line. But the Word spoken out of your mouth has the power to create what you say it. The more you say it, the more your faith will increase, and your circumstances will change.

Instead of telling yourself, "I'm sick," "I got issues," "my mother was like this," or "I'll never be anything," begin to tell yourself what God says. Instead of calling your kids and your spouse "dumb" or "stupid," begin to say what God says. Do this, and you will create the world He desires for you. Your circumstances will change.

Instead of building a partnership with the likes of Bishop Eddie Long, Bishop T.D. Jakes, Pastor Creflo Dollar or Pastor Joel Osteen, and accepting what they say about you, *confess who you are.* Tell yourself, "I'm healed; I'm delivered. My children are blessed; in school, they function at the head and not the tail. My every need is met; I am prosperous. God has given me the desires of my heart, the devil is under my feet, and no weapon formed against me will prosper." Say it and you will see that the creative power of your tongue can change your life.

When Jesus hung from the cross, He was naked. But He was "naked and unashamed." He was *willing* to be naked and unashamed with you and me in mind. The Bible says that He made Himself of no reputation because of His love for us; He was unashamed no matter what the circumstances, because even while we were sinners, He was willing to die for us.

The truth about how He hung on the cross is also important when we take a candid look at our lives. When we look at the mistakes that we've made, the generational messes we have been born into, it's important for us to establish our righteousness in Him so that we can stand wherever we are in life and be "naked and unashamed."

Once you accept Jesus' sacrifice, according to Romans 10:9 you are saved. There's no mistake, no fear or insecurity that can change that. Some of your family members may differ...but ask them about their past. We need to be positive about ourselves, and the bottom line is this: your soul needs to be saved. The problem with our churches today is that they are not teaching salvation. The Apostle Paul makes a powerful statement when he speaks of "...one thing that I do forget, those things that are behind and I press." So you have to keep pressing; keep getting up.

Too many so-called Christians are just "playing church." That sounds harsh, but unfortunately, it's all too true. When our actions don't match the guidelines set forth for Christians in the Bible, then we are reduced to simply feigning religion, "playing church."

There's a huge difference between being religious and being a Christian. Being religious is simply following a list of "do's and don'ts," usually when it's convenient, and because you have been taught that this is the proper or acceptable way to behave. But living that way is just playing church. If you think that's pleasing to God, you're only deceiving yourself.

Being a Christian means that everything you do or refrain from doing is because you truly love the Lord and care whether or not you are pleasing Him. Being a Christian means that you want to be like Christ and to serve His purposes. Being a Christian means leaving your selfish, worldly desires behind and staying focused on Jesus, on what He wants you to do, and who He wants you to become. There is a world of difference between being a Christian and just playing church.

Jesus said, "Why do you call Me, Lord, Lord, and do not {practice} what I tell you? For everyone who comes to Me and listens to My words {in order to heed their teaching} and does them, I will show you what he is like: He is like a man building a house, who dug and went down deep and laid a foundation upon the rock; and when a flood arose, the torrent broke against that house and could not shake or move it, because it had been securely built. But he who merely hears and does not practice doing My words is like man who built a house on the ground without a foundation, against which the torrent burst, and immediately it collapsed and fell, and the breaking and ruin of that house was great," (Luke 6:46-49). Don't be deceived; you will reap eternal destruction.

Make the decision right now, not to merely listen to the Word but, to do what it says. Stop "playing" church. Accept Jesus in your life today. It will be the best decision you have ever made.

Jesus said, "...I have come that they may have life, and have it to the fullest," (John 10:10). Have you discovered the joy and peace of personally accepting Jesus' invitation to life? Perhaps you have believed in the existence of God and His Son and have tried to live a good life, but have never consciously invited Him to be your Lord and Savior. No matter who you are, no matter what you have done, at this very moment you can make the decision of a lifetime. Jesus is knocking at the door of your heart, offering you the same wonderful life millions through the centuries have received with life-changing results. He has already paid the penalty for our sins; this is His amazing gift, freely given to each of us.

God loves you and wants to have a personal relationship with you. If you have never accepted Christ, you can be sure you will spend eternity with Jesus in Heaven. It doesn't matter who you are or what you've done. Jesus loves you personally. He died so *you* can have eternal life.

Let us pray and repent: "Lord Jesus, I have done things that are wrong (sins). I repent of (turn away from) my sins. I ask You to come into my heart; wash me with Your blood. I make You my Lord and Savior. Oh Lord, You are now more than my God; You are my Heavenly Father and I'm going to serve You all the days of my life. Jesus is my Lord. Amen."

If you prayed that prayer in true sincerity, the Bible says you have been born again. "Therefore, if anyone is in Christ, he is a new creation; the old is gone, the new has come," (2 Corinthians 5:17). Once you are born again, the Holy Bible says you have been transformed; you have been made into a new creature. Every sin you have ever committed, no matter how bad, is now completely, totally, one-hundred-percent forgiven and forgotten by God.

"For such are false apostles, deceitful workers, transforming themselves into apostles of Christ. And no wonder! For Satan himself transforms himself into an angel of light. Therefore it is no great thing if his ministers also transform themselves into ministers of righteousness, whose end will be according to their works."

—2 Corinthians 11:13-15

JUDGMENT DAY IS COMING

CHAPTER 9
JUDGMENT DAY IS COMING

Your snake–your pastor—will not be the one who judges you when Judgment Day arrives. I am very much aware that he or she may portray themselves as the one who can be the judge, but Reuben Armstrong has a special report.

Are you ready when Christ comes to judge the world? "And as it is appointed for men once to die, but after this the judgment," (Hebrews 9:27). We have two scheduled appointments; they're not like the doctor's appointment you scheduled the other day. These two appointments we will definitely keep: death and judgment. Judgment day is certain. There is no escaping it. Every one of us will be there for this final appointment. "For we must all appear before the judgment seat of Christ that each one may receive the things done in the body, according to what he has done in the body, whether good or bad. Knowing, therefore, the terror of the Lord, we persuade men," (2 Corinthians 5:10-11).

No one will be excluded; we all will stand before the Lord and be judged. Some people think that they are being judged right now. Some say that we are not going to have a judgment day. Well, here's breaking news: beware of those foolish people because they are liars and they are deceiving you. According to my reading of the Bible, we will not know when Judgment Day is coming. "Therefore you also be ready, for the Son of Man is coming at an hour you do not expect," (Matthew 24:44). "But the day of the Lord will come as a thief in the night, in which the heavens will pass away with a great noise, and the elements will melt with fervent heat; both the earth and the works that are in it will be burned up. Therefore, since all these things will be dissolved, what manner of persons ought you to be in holy conduct and godliness," (2 Peter 3:10-11).

We must be very serious about the Judgment. "For we shall all stand before the judgment seat of Christ. For it is written 'As I live, says the Lord, every knee shall bow to me, and every tongue shall confess to God.' So then each of us shall give an account of himself to God," (Romans 14:10-12).

You may be asking yourself what the Judgment will be like. I'm glad you asked. "Then I saw a great white throne, and Him who sat on it, from whose face the earth and the heaven fled away. And there was found no place for them. And I saw the dead, small and great, standing before God, and books were opened. And another book was opened, which is the Book of Life. And the dead were judged according to their works, by the things written in the books... And anyone not found written in the Book of Life was cast into the lake of fire with the devil, who deceived them, cast into the lake of fire and brimstone where the beast and false prophet are. And they shall be tormented day and night forever and ever," (Revelation 20:11-12, 15, 10). That sounds very scary to me.

Like I always say on my talk show, "...this is *real* talk." Personally, I don't want to be cast into the lake of fire. I think Bishop Eddie Long, Pastor Creflo Dollar, Pastor Joel Osteen, and Bishop T.D. Jakes will be if they don't repent.

You need to ask yourself whether your name is in the Book of Life. No, not the earthly book of life the snake-pastors proclaim. I mean the real Book of Life. Your eternal life in Heaven depends on it being there.

The Lord is omniscient. He knows all things. There is nothing hidden from Him, "...and there is no creature hidden from His sight, but all things are naked and open to the eyes of Him to whom we must give an account," (Hebrews 4:13).

The Lord will make no mistakes in the Judgment. "For God will bring every deed into judgment, including every hidden thing, whether good or evil," (Ecclesiastes 12:14). We can't hide any secrets from God. He knows everything about each of us.

Our Lord tells us to "Enter the narrow gate, for wide is the gate and broad is the way that leads to destruction, and there are many who go in by it. Because narrow is the gate and difficult is the way which leads to life and there are few who find it," (Matthew 7:13-14).

At Judgment, there will be two groups of people: those lost and those saved. In which group will you be? Do not be fooled or tricked concerning Judgment Day. Jesus says, "Not everyone who says to Me, Lord, Lord, shall enter the kingdom of heaven, but he who does the will of my Father in heaven." On that day, many–including Bishop T.D. Jakes, Bishop Eddie Long, Pastor Creflo Dollar and Pastor Joel Osteen among others—will say, Lord, Lord, have we not prophesied in your name, cast out demons in your name, and done many wonders in your name? "And then I will declare to them, I never knew you; depart from me, you who practice lawlessness," (Matthew 7:21-23).

Many will be shocked, amazed and terrified to learn that their sincerity, good works, and prayers will be to no avail if they have left out the essential component of *obedience to God's will*. Neither the church in which you are a member, your denomination, or your good works matter. What matters is whether you believe in the Lord Jesus Christ and obey God's commands.

How wise it is to obey the will of God today! No human creed written by man or a convention of men will do us any good. God will not accept any excuses. Being religious is not enough; doing good works is not enough; preaching is not enough. We must submit to the obedience—not of our own will—but to God's will, or else we will hear the Lord say, "I never knew you, depart from me," (Matthew 7:23).

The Lord's judgment will be final; there will be no appeal. You may feel you are in court, but at judgment there'll be no plea bargain, no district attorney, and no lawyer to argue your case. The Lord's judgment will be final. There will be no appeal; there is no higher court. There will only be two verdicts: "I never knew you, depart from me." (Matthew 7:23 or "Well done, good and faithful servant...enter into the joy of your Lord," (Matthew 25:21). Everyone's number one priority in this life should be to be prepared to meet the Lord in judgment.

You can't blame your mom, your dad, your sisters or brothers like we are doing in our earthly life. If we miss Heaven and end up in Hell, we can only blame ourselves. Remember, there will not be a second chance. We have to get it right the first time. I want you to personally examine yourself and ask this question: "Am I ready for Judgment Day when the Lord returns?"

"Prepare to meet your God," (Amos 4:12).

We must be prepared for Judgment Day.

FINAL WORDS TO BISHOP LONG, BISHOP JAKES, PASTOR DOLLAR AND PASTOR OSTEEN

CHAPTER 10
FINAL WORDS TO BISHOP LONG, BISHOP JAKES, PASTOR DOLLAR AND PASTOR OSTEEN

Please repent and ask God to forgive you for leading his children astray. You may think that repentance means when you feel sorrow, guilt, or shame for sin; but this is not repentance. The Bible says, "For godly sorrow produces repentance leading to salvation, not to be regretted; but the sorrow of the world produces death" (2 Corinthians 7:10). If one is only sorry he got caught, then this will not lead to repentance. Godly sorrow helps bring on repentance. Repentance is not sorrow for sin, but one cannot repent without being sorry he has sinned. "Let the wicked forsake his way…let him return to the Lord, and He will have mercy on him…for He will abundantly pardon" (Isaiah 55:7). In repentance, one must first understand he has sinned, feel sorrow for the sin and then stop and turn away from that sin.

"Truly, the times of this ignorance God overlooked, but now commands all men everywhere to repent" (Acts 17:30). All people are commanded to repent. It is not possible for anyone, except our Lord, to live a sin-free life, but this is no excuse for our sinning. "If we say we have no sin, we deceive ourselves; and the truth is not in us" (1 John 1:8). We also read in 2 Peter 3:9, "The Lord is not slack concerning His promise, as some count slackness, but is longsuffering toward us, not willing that any should perish but that all should come to repentance." It is God's goodness that should lead us to repentance. "Or do you despise the riches of His goodness, forbearance, and longsuffering, not knowing the goodness of God leads you to repentance?" (Romans 2:4).

Paul says, "Shall we continue in sin that grace may abound? Certainly not!" (Romans 6:1-2). To show our repentance we are to "Therefore bear fruits worthy of repentance" (Matthew 3:8). Why should we repent of sins? "For the wages of sin is death" (Romans 6:3). Spiritual death is separation from God in eternity. Jesus says, "I tell you no, but unless you repent you will all likewise perish" (Luke 13:3). To Bishop Long, Bishop Jakes, Pastor Osteen and Pastor Dollar unless you repent you cannot enter in to the kingdom of Heaven, but you will eternally suffer the torments of Hell. We must give up our sin and "Therefore do not let sin reign in your mortal body" (Romans 6:12).

Repentance is a change of heart, which results in a change of actions for the better. Without repentance we cannot receive forgiveness and be saved. Where we spend eternity, in Heaven or Hell is determined by our repentance. All of Heaven is anxious for us to repent. Jesus says, "Likewise, I say to you, there is joy in the presence of the angels of God over one sinner who repents" (Luke 15:10).

LETTERS TO THE AUTHOR

THE PIMP AND THE HUSTLING SPIRIT

Submitted By:
Pastor Heloise Sulyans-Gibson: Chaplain

Tend (nurture, guard, guide, and fold) the flock of God that is [your responsibility], not by coercion or constraint, but willingly; not dishonorable motivated by the advantages and profits [belonging to the office], but eagerly and cheerfully, 1 Peter 5:2 Amplified Bible.

There is an unseen epidemic that is overtaking many of the churches in our land of the free and the home of the brave. A nation built on the premise of freedom of religion. Where men and women could boldly, and proudly, speak the Word God. Where prayer once started the school day with fellowship and not metal detectors! Today, if you say the word God you are scorned and frowned upon. This is not the only thing that has changed. I have been watching this new disease affect many in the body of Christ's, self-esteem, self worth and ability to trust those in leadership. Lack of knowledge maintains the confusion and hurt. My people are destroyed for lack of knowledge. Hosea 4:6a Many in the body of Christ are not studying the Word of God enough. (Study and be eager and do your utmost to present yourself to God approved (tested by trial) a workman who has no cause to be ashamed, correctly analyzing and accurately dividing (rightly handling and skillfully teaching) the Word of Truth.) 2 Timothy 2:15 Amplified Bible

When you take time to study the Word of God you are equipped, trained and in tuned to hear the voice of God. The sheep that are My own hear and are listening to My voice; and I know them, and they follow Me. John10: 27 Amplified Bible

Your discernment is increased; your eyes are sharp as an eagle soaring above the valley of the dry bones and all the player haters. Your Holy Ghost directs you when something is not right. Just like the robot in Lost in Space yells, "Warning, warning, Will Robinson," your Holy Ghost will alert you as you pause for a second before you begin warring in your heavenly language, which is your weapon of warfare, speaking in tongue. This will position you for dealing with drama for you're now ready! I have learned in life to view every situation

159

with either my right hand or left hand. Is this a situation of love or confusion and I act accordingly.

What is this epidemic? I call it the Pimp and Hustling Spirit doing business in the church. This spirit is cunning and shrewd, with the gift of communication on the level of a first rate sales person; the same sales person that when you come to their office you see all their awards and plaque for state and regional sales. They are always trying to get you to give through the various forms of manipulation, rationalization and justification. It is just another form of bullying. Let me share with you some of the times I have had to encounter this spirit and how it affected me through various attacks, yet, Jesus has delivered me from this spirit.

I was at a joint service sitting on the pulpit in my regular seat. It came time for the offering. Bring all the tithes (the whole tenth of your income) into the storehouse, that there may be food in My house, and prove Me now by it, says the Lord of hosts, if I will not open the windows of heaven for you and pour you out a blessing, that there shall not be room enough to receive it. Malachi 3:10 Amplified Bible

Before the people were permitted to come and give, a leader walked up to the microphone and declared, as she looked at all the leaders on the pulpit, "I want $100 dollars from every minister sitting up here on the pulpit.

If you are a minister, you are supposed to have money. Come and bring the money right to my hand."

I knew that I was an ordained Evangelist, unemployed and every penny I had was put back into the prison ministry, since the church informed me that they had no money for this ministry. When God called me to prison ministry, while sitting in a New York State prison, He instructed me to start a pen pal encouragement, food package, and a job outreach. I did not say to God I do not have the money, so I cannot do it! I said. "Lord, this is Your ministry and I know You will provide everything that is needed!" And my God will liberally supply ({a} fill to the full) your every need according to His riches in glory in Christ Jesus. Phil 4:19.

She began calling the ministers; some had post-dated their check to appease the leader. I got up from my seat, walked right up to the leader and said, "My Pastor got it for me!"

She looked at him and he said, "It's okay."

While I had been waiting, the spirit of rejection was attacking me. I heard, "You ain't no evangelist! You do not have any money. You have no power! You are nobody! You are a failure! If you are a minister, you are supposed to have $100. You only have $5.00. What do you think God will do with your $5.00? You don't have enough."

I said, "I am the widow woman with the mite! God knows my heart! I am not a failure! God called me, not man! I will get up out of my seat and approach the leader because I have nothing to be ashamed about, I am not afraid. God always leaves a way out. Speak the Word and the enemy will flee." When I held my head high, walked to the leader, and spoke the truth I was free and at peace.

One Sunday a guest speaker was brought in to inform the church of how to become a millionaire. Already, I was not feeling this because I called myself a billionaire. Nine days earlier, I had begun a fast of no meat! This was truly a challenge; I am a full figured woman of God! I was committed to complete the fast so I asked a friend, who was a vegetarian, to go food shopping with me. I got vegetables, fruit, dry beans, garlic wrap and several recipes. When I entered church, the Holy Spirit was already in alert mode. I heard warning, warning Pastor Gibson, danger, danger! I sat down and participated in Bible study. They were discussing how people would not accept you when God has called you. I thought this was what the world does, not some of the church folks!

Service begins and I sit on the pulpit. While the praise and worship is going forth, a leader walks up and tells me "Baby we do not wear pants on the pulpit."

I looked at her and informed her, "My Pastor and I went through this last year, and he informed me that the pants have nothing to do with my anointing."

She was not expecting that for an answer. "When we have joint services in the future, protocol is not to wear pants on the pulpit."

I said, "No problem. If you want, I'll go sit down in the pews. I am healed from the rejection spirit!"

She said, "No, no baby, that is alright."

I sat down and began to ask "Lord, what's going on?"

I was not praising the Lord in my radical way, so she returned and said, "Baby, it's okay if you get up and praise Him like you normally do." Warning, Warning, Pastor Gibson!

Announcements began and I informed my Pastor that the Prison Ministry has an announcement. He looked at me and motioned for me to write out the announcement. I told him, "You know that I never write anything down for the prison ministry, that I am led by the Holy Spirit on how to make the announcement for the members to truly understand the need!" He was not happy with this statement. I looked at his face, fanned my hand and said, "Never mind!"

He understood there might be a problem and said, "Go Ahead!"

I had been preparing for over two months for the

annual Advocacy Day in Albany. This was a statewide meeting of over one hundred and fifty secular organizations and three ministries who were working to change many state policies and laws concerning women in prison. This year we were requesting Merit Time for Women of Domestic Violence. New York State does not have a self-defense law. Many of the women in prison for domestic violence had never had any criminal history before this arrest. Majority of them suffer with depression and post-traumatic stress syndrome, because they were continuously battered. Some of the sentences are twenty to life, thirty-three to life and life in prison.

Women are losing their rights to their children for life due to New York State Adoption and Safe Families Act (ASFA). In our nation, 8.3 million children have parents under correctional supervision either in prison, jail on probation or parole. One and a half million children have a parent in a state or federal prison. If a child is in foster care, fifteen of twenty-two months, the agency is required by law to file a proceeding to terminate parental rights. The majority of women in New York State are doing thirty-six months or more. There were several problems to these issues; many of the caseworkers have a double caseload from fifteen to thirty clients, or more. The caseworker is not able to bring a child up for a visit.

The women at the facility have counselors and by law they are permitted to make a phone call to her child or children. Many counselors will ask if the individual has any money in her account. If she says no, she is denied the phone call that by law is permitted. When the judge reviews the termination records they see, no record of the mother's visits, or phone calls and they assume that the mother wants nothing to do with the child or children. I heard the Holy Spirit instruct me to begin to share how I did not see my son for two years because I would not subject him nor my senior citizen mother to a twelve-hour ride upstate New York to see me. While I was telling my testimony, the tears began rolling down my face as I pleaded with the members to show the women that they care and give an offering to the prison ministry today! My Pastor told me to tell them to give after the service was over at the door as they were leaving. I sat down and then the Word went forth. The speaker was telling the members how to see the manifestation of them speaking in tongue. All during the sermon I was just weeping on the pulpit as the LORD spoke, 'Don't worry Jeremiah; they don't take care of the least of them. I got this! Don't worry Jeremiah they don't take care of the least of them. I got this!'

Tithes and offering were called for; my Pastor tossed me $25 dollars for the prison ministry. Instructions were given to first place your tithes and offering in the basket then come to the woman of God for she wanted to anoint the people and have an offering for her. I still am hearing, 'Don't worry Jeremiah, they don't take care of the least of them. I got this!' Next the leader requests every member give a $20 fellowship offering. When all this was done another announcement was made that after the service was over the woman of God wants to impart 10 keys to prosperity and please meet her after service.

After service I was sitting in the back waiting for the prison ministry offering. While I was waiting, a woman who had given a word about me crying earlier to the church came to me again and said, "God said you need to stop crying about your past" I informed her that this was not why I was crying, I was crying for all those women were still locked in prison and people don't seem to care about them. You have to watch the people trying to give you a Word. When she had stated in the service that God said stop crying and do not look back, I knew that was the enemy trying to steal the power of truth of my experience. It is because of my time in prison that I have a fire and zeal for the many who are sitting waiting for the church to come and visits. She then gave me $2 saying she had no more money. I watched as people went down stairs after service for the impartation. I received $36 for the prison ministry that day. I left because another church told me to come for they had $50 for the prison ministry.

Later that night one of my spiritual daughters called. I asked her what the ten keys to prosperity were. She said, "Ma, I don't want to tell you what happened?"

I said, "Stop playing and tell me what happened."

She informed me that the woman was selling her t-shirts that said millionaire, CD's, DVD's and vitamins and getting people to sign up to be members. I asked her, "So how much money do you guess was going around there?"

"About $2, 500."

I asked her about the hour of power they held after I left. "Did they take an offering?"

"Yes!"

"Did they take an offering for the speaker?"

"Yes!"

When I heard all of that I said, "Lord why did you clean me up from crack to only see the pimp and the hustling spirit here in the church."

The Lord said, "So you could see how this spirit is taking the church."

I recently went on a retreat for several days to a Christian Camp Ground. I was sitting in a service when I heard the man of God say tonight we are celebrating 777. I do not know what it means prophetically or in the spirit realm. I understand that when the planets align there is something to it. I said here we go again. When people of God want to talk about planets aligning this is a warning, warning Pastor Gibson. We are not supposed to be dealing with astrology or witchcraft. Then, he announced that they could ask for an offering of $777 but they will ask for an offering of $77 and 77 people. He then said, "If you give the $77, God will heal you. I sat up and told the Pastor beside me here we go again. Making people think that God will only heal you if you have $77, when the other night at the service God touched my legs and I am now using the cane less. I need to walk to strengthen my muscles in my leg now and all I had that night for offering was $3.00. He proceeded on saying there is someone in here who needs $70,000 for a house if you give the $77 you will get your house. What happened to letting the Spirit of God speak to the hearts of the children of God to give? I had enough and got up to leave when they had 40 people at the altar. They were holding back the Word until they got 77 people. All I heard was fleecing the flock!

This is not the only way the Pimp and Hustling spirit is operating in the church. Woe to him who builds his house by unrighteousness and his upper chambers by injustice, who uses his neighbor's service without wages and does not give him his pay for his work. Jeremiah 22:13

There are members who have been asked by the Pastor to be administrative assistant for the church in return for a small wage. They work long hours seven days a week and yet never receive the pay for their wages. When they ask the Pastor, they are informed, 'we do not have the money.' You, the administrative assistant, fill out the bank deposits, pay the bills and keep all the books. What's wrong with this picture? You are not the type of person to be confrontational because you are a people pleaser and are fearful that you will not be liked any more. Looking for love and validation from the leader and not God is wrong. Psychological abuse is rampant in the church this is all a part of the Pimp and Hustling spirit. Many come to serve in the house of the Lord and are being used, and their self esteem and self worth are being damaged.

Let's talk about the members that pay their tithes and offering all the time. They support the church in any way asked and even come up with ideas to increase membership and economic growth for their home of worship. They look at their church as their home even clean it on Saturday. One day they decide they want to have an event at the church and ask the Pastor. He informs them that they have to pay $500 to use the church. Yet, this member has sown over $60,000 in the ministry over the years.

Many think that this is the way to get money from the members yet all this does is cause confusion in the body. The world has entered the church with the belief system that the church is a business. The last I looked it is a hospital where the lost and the broken hearted are suppose to be set free from the bondages of life from the hurts of manipulation, justification, rationalization, lying, and the list is endless. What happened to just speaking the truth to the people. 'Members our cost of operating has increased; these are our bills for the month.' We need to be praying, fasting and changing our lives to be more Christ like for the blessings of God to be manifested in our lives.

I can truly say game recognizes game, many in the body have not gotten rid of the pimp and hustling residues in their lives and many are being infected with this destructive behavior and spirit. I want to encourage the body of Christ study the Word, build up your spirit man as you eat and chew on the Word. If you do this when you hear the Rev. Buzzard in the land you will not fall for the trickery. You will be led by the Hoy Spirit. We know that when the Holy Spirit speaks to you to give, it will not be a struggle. I do not know about you, but Jesus never had $500, $300, $200, $100, or $50 prayer lines. Prayers are free—just pray and stay connected to the true

Vine. For out of His fullness (abundance) we have all received [all had a share] and we all supplied with one grace after another and spiritual blessing upon spiritual blessing and even favor upon favor and gift [heaped] upon gift. John 1:16

I APPLAUD YOU, MR. ARMSTRONG

Submitted By:
The Honorable James David Manning, PhD
ATLAH World Ministries

The first commandment of Satan is "through your greed ye shall prosper," Gen.3:1-7 and Matt. 4:1-11. This first evil commandment was spoken by Satan as a snake from a tree in the Garden of Eden. Perhaps the place from which Satan spoke was a prepared oak creation auditorium, in other words; Satan had set up a trap with all the bells and whistles to lure Eve to his side of town.

Sometime later in the scheme of continuing his sermons, Satan preached another powerful message of so-called "blessings from a rock," but this time his sermon was to the Son of God. He spent several days in a one-man conference on prosperity and church growth. Satan's basic sermon to Jesus was you can rule the world by using my version of Your Word, Matt.4:8-11. In other words, Satan had the Bible in his hand, he was preaching Holy Ghost verses, but he was twisting them out of context, and he was lying through his fangs. Thank God, Jesus knew when He heard His word being used by a liar.

Mr. Reuben Armstrong's call and rebuke of these new snakes who now preach from pulpits is "spot on Biblical" in identifying the one note sermon of greed. Satan's claim is that his version of the Bible will set you free, make you rich like me, happy, successful, powerful, and enjoying life everyday, Matt. 4:1-11.

You will notice that in Satan's first sermon, he did not use a strange doctrine or idea that was not akin to the then known authorized Word of God. He gave Eve a more acceptable interpretation of a word that she was very familiar with, Gen. 3:1-6.

Satan promised Eve would be as powerful as God almighty, and she would be able to have all that she desired, if she applied Satan's version of God's word.

He also lied about the outcome in addition to the poor interpretation of God's word. Mrs. Eve had been sternly instructed by Mr. Adam that she would die if she advanced to or ate from the Tree of the Knowledge of Good and Evil, Gen. 3:1-6.

Now, please take notice that the most obvious way to

demonstrate greed is through the stomach. Eve was invited to eat by Satan appealing to her lower nature and the greed of her flesh. Satan realized he had a winner by appealing to the greed and lust nature of man, and likewise invited Jesus to eat to satisfy His hunger. This second invitation was offered many years later in the wilderness while Jesus was fasting and praying as He prepared to lead His Church, Gen. 3:1-7 and Matt. 4:1-4.

Now there are several things I desire you to observe. One, is the instinct of greed is a latent yet powerful enough tool to bring even the strongest man to the Church of Satan and the twisted gospel of greed.

Greed must be powerful otherwise, Satan would not have used it against Jesus when he suggested to Him to turn the stones into bread, and eat and be filled.

I have noticed that most non-religious people are never interested in or subject to become victims of today's beguiling preachers. By that, I mean you must first have some elementary relationship with the Word of God before you can be persuaded to listen to the twisted interpretation in a manner that will feed your greed. In other words, you must qualify as both weak of mind and greedy of spirit before believing Satan's version of the gospel of prosperity and enjoying life everyday.

You will notice like Satan's sermon in the wilderness of temptation with Jesus in Matt. 4:1-11, today's snakes are skilled at twisting the Word; but only to those who are religious and have an elementary acquaintance with scripture. Seldom do you find people of reasonable education and honesty giving any attention to these preachers, like Joel Osteen, T.D. Jakes, Creflo Dollar, and Eddie Long.

The names that Mr. Armstrong has focused on are major players in the Gospel/Promise Prosperity shell game. They say, "You give to me and God will bless you." Their preamble to the class of the blessed of God; "is you can have what you say, it only takes faith and some seed money. Like the farmer sows a seed and reaps a harvest, you too can sow a seed and reap a great harvest of money to make you rich."

So, the greedy and the gullible empty their pockets and spend their rent money like an addicted gambler at the race track, wagering his bets to place, win or show.

These addicted, greedy Christians, and these players like Eddie Long and T.D Jakes keep the hype and the promises of the great life flowing like 99 bottles of beer on the wall. They pump up the theatrics in the church building, hit you with powerful music and singing, have others give testi-lying testimonies and then they get up and preach as if the sky is falling about how God wants you to be prosperous.

That most dangerous Black Mambo snake called Joel Osteen, acts like he doesn't even have to go to the bathroom he is so perfect and blessed.

That Joel Osteen is the most notorious Christian hustler in Texas today, and that is saying a lot because all things are big in Texas.

I would like to ask all pastors this one question: 'Do you really believe that God is blessing Joel Osteen more than the average pastor?' By that, I mean, do you believe he lives a more sacred life, prays more effectively, and is more deserving of God's blessing than the pastor down the street?

The answer of course is what the queried pastors will give, but I am here to testify, Joel Osteen is just a better hustler than the faithful pastors.

Please take notice of the kind of sermon that Satan preached to Jesus in Matt. 4:1-11. You will notice that Satan always used authorized scripture in the wilderness temptation sermon. Yet, in every word of Satan's prophecy to Jesus was that He would have a great life if Jesus, simply followed Satan's interpretation of the authorized Holy scriptures. Not once did Satan ever tell Jesus about servanthood or any of the noble things of integrity and righteousness. He just kept feeding him the prosperity, power messages, and living life good everyday.

Often people write to me and say that T.D. Jakes is a man of God, that I should take the Bible, and bless people the way he does. Well, he may be a man of God, but he is certainly not a man of the God of the Bible. Perhaps his god is Baal, Chemosh, Ashteroth, or some unknown god, but not Jesus, Judg. 2:13, I Kings 11:33, Acts 17:23, Matt. 7:21.

Two things are evident here and need to be said about such advice. First, only people who are greedy for filthy lucre would ever go anywhere near a sermon that T.D. Jakes would preach. You don't go looking for a bull in a china shop. What they interpret is blessed preaching are messages of dope, rather than eternal hope.

Secondly, Jakes knows that he is dealing with thieves who dress up, carry Bibles, and profess it is God's will that they be whatever their new Pentecostal jargon claims them to be. Jakes has discovered this, and it has made him a rich man.

Indeed, Jakes, Dollar, Long, Osteen, and others have become a type of new drug dealer in the ghettos of Christianity.

I applaud you, Mr. Armstrong, for your courageous work, keep the sacred work going, and tell the truth at the cost of your own life, Matthew 10:39.

A FINAL WORD FROM THE AUTHOR

A FINAL WORD FROM THE AUTHOR

This book was not written to divide the flock, but to shed light on issues that most refuse to face for whatever reason. I know within the Spirit of God that judgment is approaching the House of God. While everyone else is focusing on prosperity and new beginnings, I can't help but hear the cry of WOE! I'm not looking nor searching for instant fame or glory but I'm just one of a few that God has chosen to cry loud against SIN! We made His house a DEN OF THIEVES! Rather than conforming the world to the Church, we've conformed to the world and have kindled the anger of God! Holiness is still right and a lifestyle we cannot afford to turn away from. The WORD declares that Judgment begins at the House of God, so regardless who it is, and what the stakes are we must allow God to be God. While we pray and cover one another, we must realize that SIN is SIN and stinks in the nostrils of God! Yes, he that is without SIN let him cast the first stone, but he who tries to hide behind the cross and allow the anointing of God to be pimped, let that man be exposed! Yes, all have sin and come short to the Glory of God, but when that person becomes an idol rather than an example God must bring that person down.

My brothers and sisters in Christ, I know many of you have been hurt by so-called "men of God."

God never intended for the church to be a business for pastors. Many of these men and women have essentially become CEOs of large corporations, which masquerade as churches. Ultimately, no one is benefiting from what they are teaching. They are false prophets, making promises of wealth untold while draining the resources of both true believers and nonbelievers alike. They're selling greed under the banner of prosperity. Some pastors even boast about their cars and houses in their sermons; they seem to see prayer as a means to justify their greed, instead of a way to come to know God.

Millions upon millions of people worldwide are being deceived by these false prophets and are under the spell of every word that fall from their mouths. Millions, even billions, of dollars are being spent by believers, many of whom simply can't afford to support these false preachers.

Satan is a master of deception. I cannot say this with enough emphasis. His lies and deceits will make you believe him if you're not grounded in the Holy Word of God.

I beseech you; beware of the teachings of these snakes. Test what you hear against the Word of God. Do not take a preacher's word for what he says; they are adept at quoting scripture, twisting it and perverting its meaning. Read for yourself. Pray for guidance from God, Jesus and the Holy Spirit so that you will be enlightened to the truth, as God would have you see it.

Christ made it clear that Satan would search us out, look for our weaknesses and concentrate on those areas of our lives to lull us into a sense of false security. This makes us even more susceptible to being lead astray without even realizing it.

God is not asleep. He is very much aware that Bishop Eddie Long, Pastor Creflo Dollar, Pastor Joel Osteen and Bishop T.D. Jakes are leading their flock astray, that their ministries focuses on greed, wealth, fame and fortune.

The sad thing is that older ministers, who should know better, and young upcoming ministers are following in the footsteps of these so-called "men of God," and helping lead others to the pits of hell. Pastors should focus more on teaching about faith and other aspects of the Bible, not on money, success, and worldly blessings. The majority of these pastors are deceiving people, pulling the wool over the eyes of many people around the world. They would have us believe they have direct contact with the Man above. It's weird how these so-called men of God confess the privileges they have with God while continuing to fly in their million dollar jets and having sex with whores.

It's not surprising that the wives of Bishop Eddie Long, Pastor Joel Osteen, Bishop T.D. Jakes and Pastor Creflo Dollar seldom travel with their husbands. They know their husbands are not right with God and that they are deceiving millions. They know their husbands are milking billions and billions of dollars from true and un-true believers. Sadly, the mighty dollar has taken over the world, and these women have become accustomed to wealth; they'd be nuts to leave their snakes. Can you imagine how these preachers' wives can take all the abuse? Their husbands are rarely at home; they know their husbands are having sex with church folks; many of them are abused, verbally and physically.

It's not just those pimps we have to be careful in handling. Church folks also affect the people in the church. Some are not there to praise the Lord; some attend church because it's a tradition. Others are there to kill, steal and destroy; some are there trying to get a hand into the pastors' pocket or to satisfy the pastors' sexual wants. Be careful; some of these "Holy-Ghost-fire-filled" women will cut your throat over these pastors and their money. These women can make you think you are on the streets, but most people on the street treat you better than these church folks.

We, as a people, have to stay prayed up; we have to build our own personal relationships with God. You can't know another man's true intentions.

Our world is changing every single day. Have you ever driven from block to block and wondered why you see three or four churches on a single street? It's because religion has become a business in today's world. These churches are not trying to save your soul or teach you how to have a relationship with God. Instead they focus on three things: money, power and sex.

They know that if they can take scriptures and twist them for their own use, the normal jackasses will reach deep into their pockets and donate to their personal financial empires. Their formula is simple. They entice you into their church where you'll hear some good music. You'll also listen to somebody telling you to pray and God will take care of everything. If this were true, why are there members in that very church or that church's community who are lost, homeless and hungry?

Yes, God will take care of everything. However, you have pastors who have already reaped their blessings, but who are not fulfilling the commandments of God.

I say to you, "Pray. Pray without ceasing."

Amen.

Printed in the United States
102397LV00001B/40-129/A